Christian Heritage Series
THE SANTA FE YEARS

W9-AUK-383

The Choice

Nancy Rue

BETHANY HOUSE PUBLISHERS
MINNEAPOLIS, MINNESOTA 55100

Focus on the Family books are available at special quantity discounts when purchased in bulk by corporations, organizations, churches, or groups. Special imprints, messages, and excerpts can be produced to meet your needs. For more information, contact: Resource Sales Group, Focus on the Family, 8605 Explorer Drive, Colorado Springs, CO 80920; or phone (800) 932-9123.

A Focus on the Family book
Published by Bethany House Publishers
A Ministry of Bethany Fellowship International
11400 Hampshire Avenue South
Bloomington, Minnesota 55438
www.bethanyhouse.com

Printed in the United States of America by
Bethany Press International, Bloomington, Minnesota 55438

Library of Congress Cataloging-in-Publication Data

Rue, Nancy N.
    The choice / Nancy N. Rue.
        p.   cm. — (Christian Heritage series. The Santa Fe years ; 6)
Summary: In Santa Fe, New Mexico, just before the end of World War II, twelve-year-old Will, his family and friends face many changes and have many consequential decisions to make with Jesus' help.
    ISBN 1-56179-896-7
1. World War, 1939-1945—United States—Juvenile fiction. [1. World War, 1939-1945—United States—Fiction. 2. Family life—New Mexico—Fiction. 3. Manhattan Project (U.S.)—Fiction. 4. Christian life—Fiction. 5. Santa Fe (N.M.)—History—20th century—Fiction.] I. Title.
    PZ7.R88515 Cj   2002
    [Fic]—dc21   2002000968

02 03 04 05 06 07 08 / 14 13 12 11 10 9 8 7 6 5 4 3 2 1

For Gwen Ellis,
without whom the Christian Heritage Series
would never have been born.

Chapter One

*T*he second Will Hutchinson set his foot on the first of the steps leading up to his back door, something grabbed his ankle.

Even as he gave a yell, and even as he stumbled forward and the canned ham and the box of lard flew out of the Roybal's Grocery bag he was carrying, Will knew what it was—and *who* it was.

Dumping the bag and its few remaining contents onto the top step, he reached down and clamped onto the brown hand that was still clutching his sock.

"Come out of there, Fawn," Will said. "And so help me, if that ketchup bottle got broken, you're gonna pay for it!"

A head of dark, thick-braided hair appeared from under the back stoop, and Fawn's black eyes glared at him as she jerked her hand away.

"I don't care about your old ketchup," she said, untangling her lanky arms and legs.

"You'll care about it the next time there's not enough for your meat loaf," Will said.

And then he wanted to bite his tongue off. Fawn looked ready to do it *for* him.

"I won't be eating ketchup *or* meat loaf here," she said in a voice bitter as vinegar. "I don't live here anymore, remember?"

"Who can forget?" Will said. "You keep running away from your mom to come back here and remind me every 10 seconds."

"Do not!"

Will was about to answer with the customary, "Do too!" but he *did* bite that back. Hard as it was to believe, he was pretty sure Fawn was about to cry—and he knew Fawn McHorse did everything in her power never, ever to shed a tear—especially in front of him.

If she has to start bawlin', he thought, *she's gonna blame me and start pounding on me.*

He looked around to make sure no one was close by to see what he was about to do.

If anybody sees me, he thought, *they'll think I'm a sissy or something.* It was never wise for a 12-year-old boy to look too soft.

Certain there were no witnesses, Will sat on the second-to-the-top step and patted the sun-warmed space beside him, his eyes on Fawn. She flopped down onto it, arms folded, face as long as a stretched-out rubber band.

"You gotta quit running back here," he said to her. "You got that swell guest house behind Margretta's with your mom. And now your dad's comin' home. I'd give my right arm to have my dad comin' home."

"No, you wouldn't," Fawn said. She dropped her chin into her hands, elbows drilling into her bare knees.

"Says who? My dad's been gone even longer than yours—"

He let his voice fade. Two large tears were teetering on the edges of Fawn's bottom lids, threatening to spill out, and she was doing nothing to stop them.

"I don't get it," Will said. "Your dad's due home in—" He glanced at his watch. "—two hours. You haven't seen him for two whole years. And you're cryin'?" He shook his head. "I just don't get it."

"I'm scared, okay?"

Fawn's fists were doubled, and her eyebrows were twisted into a W of anger—but her mouth was trembly, and the tears were rolling down. In the year and a half he'd known her, Will had never seen her this scared—or even half this scared.

"You really are afraid, huh?" he said. "I just don't get it."

"I think I do," said a voice behind them.

Will heard the summer sound of the screen door creaking open as his mother, Ingrid Hutchinson, stepped out with a glass of lemonade in each hand. Walking carefully around the spilled groceries, she squeezed in between them on the step and handed one glass to Will. She nudged Fawn with the other one.

"I'm not thirsty," Fawn said.

"Come on—this is the first lemonade I've made all summer," Mom said. "Besides, you have to replace all the fluids you're losing in those tears." She gave Fawn another nudge with the glass.

Fawn snatched it from her and gulped down half the lemonade before she took a breath. It made Will's face pucker just watching her. With sugar still being rationed, wartime lemonade was some pretty sour stuff.

But it didn't seem to faze Fawn. She drained the glass and handed it back to Mom. It had obviously done nothing to lighten her misery.

"She says she's scared," Will said to his mother. "Why would she be? I'd be so excited, I'd have run the whole 20 miles to Lamy by this time."

"Oh, I don't know about that." Mom brushed a wisp of almost-blond hair off her forehead and squinted at the fading late afternoon sun. "I think I'd be a little scared too, if I were Fawn."

Will grunted. "It must be something women do, then."

"I think this woman—" Mom leaned against Fawn with her shoulder, "is having trouble with all this change. Think about it." Mom spread out her fingers to count on them. "First her mother comes home from the hospital in Arizona after she'd been gone a whole year, and she's an entirely different person."

"You mean, because she can see now," Will said.

"Not only that, but—well, you haven't spent any time with her—she speaks English, which she could barely do before, and she isn't hopeless anymore." Mom's lips twitched, the way they did when she was hiding a smile. "And she's much more aware of her surroundings these days, which means Fawn can't get away with nearly the number of things she used to."

She pushed against Fawn, who turned her face away. But she didn't pitch a fit and threaten to leap off the stoop, so Will knew Mom was probably right so far.

Mom busied herself re-pinning the bundle of hair she wore at the nape of her neck as she went on. "She got used to basically having no Mom at all when her mother was blind and sick, and then she had to get used to me being her substitute mom, and now her mother is back again and they both have to adjust to a whole new way of doing things."

"But what's that got to do with her dad coming back from the war?" Will said.

Mom looked at Fawn, who was cutting her eyes sideways to see Mom without actually turning her head.

"It's hard enough making this adjustment," Mom said. "Now on top of it, her father is re-entering the picture. When he left, he wasn't the best father in the world—right, Fawn?"

No, Will thought, *because I have the best father in the world.* But he knew what his mother meant. He'd heard it from Margretta Dietrich, the Anglo supporter of the New Mexican Pueblo Indians, the lady who had looked after Fawn and her mother when Dan McHorse had been called to war. She said Dan had drunk heavily, hadn't been able to keep a job, and laughed at even the thought of believing in God and following the teachings of Christ.

"But now," Mom said, as if she'd been reading Will's thoughts, "he's written letters saying he doesn't drink anymore and has made a lot of other changes because he's become a Christian."

"That's good, though," Will said. "So what's to be scared of?"

" 'Cause what if it's all a lie?" Fawn said. She snapped around so that she was facing Will. "What if he gets here and everything goes back to the way it was before? What if he and my mother start fighting and throwing stuff at each other again? What if he goes out at night and comes back smelling like a brewery?"

"What's a brewery?" Will said.

"I don't know! It's what Margretta used to say. It's something that stinks, is all I know. And I don't want that!" Fawn turned to Mom. "Mama Hutchie, I just wanna stay here with you and Will and have it be like it was. I liked living here."

Mom nodded as she put her arm around Fawn's shoulders. "I know, Fawn. And we liked having you here."

To Will's surprise, Fawn didn't pull away and stand up and stomp her foot or, worse, lunge at Will and pound him, which was what she usually did when she didn't get what she wanted. She just sagged against Mom and stared glumly at the toes of her saddle oxfords, scuffed from being under the porch.

"What if he doesn't like me?" she said.

"*What?*" Will said. "He's your dad! He has to like you!"

Mom squeezed his arm, even as she pulled Fawn closer to her. It was her "Time to hush up, Will" signal.

"I'm different now too," Fawn said. "Aren't I?"

"Definitely," Mom said. "And all in good ways. But let me tell you something about parents: they love you no matter what." Her lips twitched as she glanced at Will. "I put up with this character here even when he's arguing my ear off."

Fawn peeked around Mom to get a look at Will, and the corners of her mouth turned up.

"Yeah, he's pretty hard to love sometimes," she said. "I guess if you can love *him,* my dad can love *me.*"

"Gee, thanks a lot!" Will said.

Mom slung her free arm around him and pulled him in. "He'll do in a pinch," she said.

To Will's relief she let go right away and stood up. She was a swell mom that way—never too much mushy stuff, especially in public.

"Why don't we walk you back to Margretta's?" Mom said. "She and your mother will be waiting for you—it's time to head for the train station."

Fawn shook her head. "You don't have to be afraid I'll run off," she said. "I think I can do this now." She stood up and smoothed a hand over her neatly parted hair. "Do I look all right?"

Does she look all right? Will thought. *Since when does Fawn care what she looks like?*

Mom complimented her on her shiny thick braids and the new plaid dress with the crisp white collar, which a few months ago Fawn wouldn't have been caught dead in. Mom *didn't* comment on the under-the-stoop dirt that punctuated each elbow and knee on the gangly arms and legs. Will rolled his eyes at the whole thing.

I'm sure not gonna act like this when my dad comes home. If *my dad comes home.* Will shook off the "if." He *was* going to come home. Hitler had died two months before, the Germans had surrendered, and the Nazis were defeated. The way things were going in the Pacific, the Japanese were sure to give up soon. Then he and Mom would be meeting *their* dad at the train in Lamy.

And I'm not gonna be scared. I'm gonna be out-of-my-mind happy!

"All right, I'm ready," Fawn said. And then she threw her arms around Mom's neck.

Will turned quickly to pick up the spilled groceries before she got any ideas about hugging *him.* He was relieved when Fawn just gave him a wave and took off around the house and up Canyon Road.

But the minute she was out of sight, Will felt a strange wisp of loneliness.

"I see popcorn in my immediate future," Mom said suddenly. "How 'bout you?"

"With butter?" Will said.

That got a twitch from her. With butter being rationed even more tightly than sugar, asking for it on his popcorn was like requesting a chunk of the moon. When she said, "Sure. Why not?" Will knew she was feeling a little Fawn-emptiness herself.

"Go up to your room and clear a path," she said. "I'll bring up a bowl."

Will nodded and made for the stairs, dropping the groceries off in the kitchen on the way. It was cool and dark inside the Hutchinson house as the sun began to set, but even the comforting coolness of the floor tiles and the white adobe walls and the smooth wooden banister didn't ease the unfamiliar feeling of being without Fawn.

She had lived with them for a year while her mother had been away being treated for an eye disease. Fawn had become as much a part of his life as Mom was, and now that she wasn't here to bug him when he was trying to do his homework, or to jump on his back when she got bored, or to come up with schemes that never failed to get him in trouble—it was almost like Mom herself had moved up the road. He was relieved when Mom came in with an Indian-made pottery bowl full of popcorn that was drenched in butter.

"We'll be eating dry toast for a week," she said. "But that's okay—we needed a treat *today*."

"Yeah," Will said. He was glad Mom was there, settling herself on the bed and leaning against the window frame, but he didn't want to talk about Fawn anymore. He looked up at the map of the Pacific on the wall and used it as an excuse to change the subject.

"How long do you think it'll be before we take Okinawa?" he said, pointing to the only island that didn't have a tiny metal airplane stuck to it. His Uncle Al, who worked in Military Intelligence, had given the plane pins to him when he'd found out Will was closely following the war against the Japanese in the Pacific and was learning all about things like PT boats and fighter pilots and soldiers parachuting behind enemy lines.

Mom looked up at the markers and ran her fingers over a few of them.

"We've taken all the rest of the islands," she said. "We've destroyed all the Japanese air bases and supply depots and built our own, right?"

Will nodded.

"So now our guys can get what they need to keep up the fight, and the Japanese can't. Why shouldn't it be soon?"

"That's what I'm thinking," Will said.

Mom tapped the picture from the cover of *LIFE* magazine, which Will had recently tacked onto the wall next to the map.

"This is a new addition," she said.

"Yeah."

"I'm seeing it everywhere. I heard they're even going to put it on a 3-cent postage stamp."

"They should!" Will said.

Both of them gazed for a minute at the now-familiar photograph of the group of soldiers planting an American flag at the top of Mt. Suribachi, a volcano on the island of Iwo Jima. During the bloody, four-day battle, 6,800 American soldiers had died trying to rout 22,000 Japanese soldiers with their machine gun nests out of holes and tunnels and caves.

But the Allies—America and her friends—had won. There was only one battle left before they attacked Japan itself. Everyone said that would mean the end of war if the Japanese would surrender. The Allies had agreed that it had to be an unconditional surrender. The future of Japan would have to be put into the hands of the Allies, just as the future of Germany and Italy were now.

Will had heard Britain's Winston Churchill say on the radio that there would be many disasters and a huge cost and a lot of suffering—but in the end there would be victory.

I just wish it would hurry up and come, Will thought.

He looked at the Bataan Peninsula on the map. He didn't have to glance at Mom to know she was studying it too. Whenever she got quiet and twirled a loose curl around her finger, the way she was doing now, he could tell she was thinking about the last place Rudy Hutchinson had been free—the last place he'd been able to send word that he was okay.

And even then it had been bad news. He and two of the New Mexico regiments of the 200th Coast Artillery had been taken prisoner by the Japanese in the Philippines right after the attack on Pearl Harbor, three and a half years before. There had been no telegram that he had died, so they clung to the hope that he was still alive, just as Will now found himself clinging to the bedspread.

He forced himself to relax his fingers and dig into the popcorn. At the thought of Dad, it turned to butter-soaked cardboard in his mouth.

Mom had shifted her eyes from the map to the window. Although the sky was still bright, the flat rooftops of the adobes were turning dark. It was the best part of a New Mexico summer day—the hour between the heat of the afternoon and the chill of the mountain night. The feel of the air was soft and dry, and Will could smell the wood fires starting in people's fireplaces.

"It's starting to cool off," Mom said. "That's one thing I don't miss about Chicago. In the summer it stayed hot and humid day and night." She seemed to drift back to her old hometown even as she talked. "Your father and your Aunt Hildy Helen and Uncle Al and I used to get down to as little clothing as the law would allow and sit on Aunt Gussie's porch chewing on ice. Of course, we never sat for long. Between your father and Hildy Helen and Al there was never a dull moment."

Will thought he could probably have told *her* the stories of their antics. He'd heard them enough times. But right now, the image of a bunch of friends gathered on a porch sent a pang through him.

Just last week he and Miguel and Abe and Olive and Fawn had sat on the porch of his house, swinging their legs and looking out at dusty Canyon Road with its quiet brown earthen buildings, feeling like the only human beings alive, and feeling fine with that.

Now, with Fawn gone, Miguel and Olive living all the way out at Mr. T.'s ranch, and Abe going to school in the summer, it wasn't the same. Time for another subject change.

But before Will could even look around for one, the window suddenly rattled, and two of the metal airplanes shook off of the wall and landed on the bed, where they danced as even the mattress trembled.

Then, as suddenly as they had started, the tremors stopped, leaving Will and his mom staring at each other.

"Again?" she said. "That's the second time this week. What is going on up there?"

"Up where?" Will said.

"Up near Los Alamos. Mr. T. says he's heard that all these earth shakings we've been feeling are coming from that area."

Will considered that. For the past several months, they'd been experiencing what they'd thought were small earthquakes. At first they'd barely been enough to knock the pictures crooked on the walls. Then, just since school had let out for the summer, they'd gotten stronger, and people in Santa Fe were beginning to complain about pottery crashing to the floor and pies being shaken off windowsills.

"This wasn't going on when we lived in Los Alamos," Mom said.

"I don't remember it that well," Will said. "I was just a kid when we left the school."

Mom's mouth did its twitchy thing.

"Yeah, you were eight—a mere baby compared to how ancient you are now."

"I was a little kid next to the students," Will said. "They treated me like I was an infant."

"Poor thing," Mom said, without a trace of sympathy. "It must have been tough, living in that beautiful place, riding horses every afternoon and every weekend, going on camping trips with your dad—"

Her voice trailed off. She and Dad had both taught at the Los Alamos Ranch School for Boys until he enlisted in the Army in 1941, and the government had later closed it down in 1943. Even talking about the school made them think of Dad and better days.

"There's no getting away from the loneliness today, is there?" Mom said. "I guess we got all built up over the victory in Europe, and now we feel let down."

"That's because it didn't do anything for *us*," Will said. "I mean, it did 'cause we're Americans and 'cause Fawn's dad got to come home. But—"

"No buts," Mom said. "We haven't gotten word that your dad's been killed, Will. *We* still have hope."

She didn't have to add that their friends Miguel and his mother, Señora Otero, had none. Miguel's father had also been in the 200th Coast Artillery, but he had died early in the war. When he and the other prisoners had been captured, they'd been forced to make a long, torturous march to the prison camp itself. Miguel's father had never made it that far.

And what about Olive? Will thought. Olive was his newest friend. Her mother had died in a factory accident while trying to help in the war effort. Right now, her father was in St. Vincent's Sanitarium, recovering from what the adults referred to in whispers as "being disturbed." All Will knew was that Olive's dad didn't believe in the war, and that after he went back to the sanitarium after a visit to Olive on a pass, she seemed quiet and distant to Will, as if she weren't quite sure she'd really seen her father at all.

"Penny for your thoughts, Son," Mom said.

Will shrugged. "I guess we're pretty lucky," he said.

"I don't think luck has a whole lot to do with it. I think it's looking to God to help us make the right choices."

Will could feel his forehead wrinkling up. Ever since the spring, he'd really been trying to concentrate on God, the way he concentrated on Fawn and Miguel and Olive—but what his mom had just said didn't quite make sense.

"What?" Mom said.

"I don't see how I have choices," he said. "If I had choices, I'd choose for Dad to come home right now!"

Mom started to answer, but she stopped, mouth open, as she stared outside.

Will crawled across the bed toward the window, his own mouth stuffed with popcorn.

"Fawn again?" he said in a butter-muffled voice.

But he, too, stopped when he got a glimpse through the screen. The popcorn stopped in his throat.

Below, there was a boy on a bicycle—a boy in a blue uniform—delivering a telegram.

✠ ⬥ ✠

Chapter Two

*A*ll the way down the stairs, as the telegram messenger pounded on the front door, Will's mom clung to his hand. He didn't pull away.

"It's not necessarily bad news," she said, chattering like a nervous chicken. "We haven't had a really bad telegram yet, so why should this be any different?"

"Maybe it means Dad's coming home," Will said.

"Maybe. Or maybe it's just a broken leg. Or pneumonia. They have wonder drugs for pneumonia now, you know."

Will nodded, but he knew she didn't think it was Dad having pneumonia any more than he did. They didn't send telegrams from prison camps telling the relatives their loved one was sick. Families only got telegrams when—

"That's right, Mom," Will said. It could be anything."

By the time they passed through the dining room and then the living room, Will wasn't sure which of their palms were sweatier, but he still didn't let go of Mom's hand, even when she opened the front door to reveal the Mexican boy in his blue uniform. In fact, when Will saw the yellow paper in his hand, he held on tighter.

"Telegram for Ingrid Hutchinson," the boy said.

He smiled. To Will, it seemed out of place at the moment—as out of place as the pink hollyhocks on the gate behind him and the pots of red geraniums on the porch beside him and everything else that had the nerve to seem normal just then.

It isn't normal to get a telegram! Will's thoughts screamed at him. *And whatever isn't normal is bad!*

Mom finished signing in the messenger's book—having finally peeled her hand away from Will's—and she stood motionless in the doorway, yellow telegram in hand, as she watched the boy pass through the portal of hollyhocks and climb onto his bicycle.

"Aren't you gonna open it?" Will said.

Mom nodded and moved with maddening slowness out to the porch, where she sank into one of the high-backed wooden chairs. Still she barely moved, but just sat with the telegram on her lap. The only motion was that of the moths fluttering around the light by the door. It was enough to make Will want to scream, "Open it! I can't stand this!"

And yet when Mom finally pulled her fingernail across the top of the envelope, Will bit his lip to keep from crying out, "No! Stop! I don't want to know!"

The next best thing was to close his eyes, which he did, tightly, until he heard an unexpected sound bubble up out of his mother's throat.

She was laughing.

"What?" Will said. "What's funny?"

"I don't know whether to hug her or throttle her."

"Who?"

"Your Aunt Hildy Helen. She's coming to stay with us—which is wonderful—but did she have to send a telegram? She scared me half to death!"

Mom leaned her head against the back of the chair and laughed again. Will didn't see the humor.

"Doesn't she know people always think their soldier's been killed when they get a telegram?" he said.

"Evidently not. She's been overseas with the Red Cross ever since we got into the war. I doubt she knows what's going on back here."

Mom dabbed at her eyes as she scanned the telegram again. Will hiked himself up onto the porch railing.

"She says she's been sent back to the States for health reasons," Mom said. "She's in California right now and they're releasing her from the hospital."

"Did she get shot?" Will asked. He didn't remember much about his father's twin sister, but if she'd actually been wounded in a battle, she could be pretty interesting.

"She doesn't say," Mom said. "But she doesn't want to go back to Chicago, and I can understand why. Aunt Gussie's passed on, Uncle Al's still with the Special Branch—there's no one for her there. I'm delighted that she wants to come here."

"Yeah," Will said.

"I hope we won't be too boring for her," Mom went on. "Uncle Al told me she's been directing military service clubs in Europe, dodging bombs all over the continent."

"Maybe that's how she got wounded," Will said. But now that he'd stopped shaking with relief, he was pretty much tired of talking about Aunt Hildy Helen.

Mom wasn't. Relief seemed to be making her *want* to chatter. "They were such a hoot, the three of them—Al, Rudy, and Hildy Helen. I think I have some pictures of them together around here someplace."

She was still talking away as she went to the closet in the dining room to pull out the shoebox where she kept the family photos. Will stifled a yawn and considered escaping up the steps while Mom's back was turned. But since there was nothing else to do, he shrugged and flopped down on the couch. Mom joined him with a handful of photographs.

"These are the ones I was thinking of," she said. She presented an already-fading picture of three people, all about 20 years old. The short, stockily built fellow with shiny black hair Will knew was Uncle Al, who was his dad's adopted brother.

Will snickered. "What's he doing dressed up like a baby?"

"We were all going to a costume party," Mom said. "See—Al was the baby, your Aunt Hildy Helen was the dad, and your father was the mom."

"Wacko," Will said.

"I don't know," Mom said, lips twitching. "I thought your father made a cute girl."

Will studied the picture. Dad looked anything but feminine, even in a big floppy hat with an ostrich plume sticking out of it and enough strings of beads to circle the planet. Dad's eyes had a mischievous glint, as if he were already planning his next trick on his sister. He was grinning in that way that Will could always see when he closed his eyes. He could almost hear him laughing, a rich, rolling sound that filled up a room.

It made Will ache inside.

"I think we'll give Hildy Fawn's old room," Mom said. "We have a little time—I can fix it up."

"How come she has to sleep in Fawn's room?" Will said. "What if Fawn has to come back here? What if her father doesn't like her or he hasn't really changed like he keeps promising he has?"

Mom pulled her eyes from the photographs and rested them softly on Will. "She won't be coming back here to live, Son," she said. "We have to accept that."

Will wasn't in an accepting mood—not then, and definitely not the next morning when, even before he had finished his fried egg sandwich, the back door flew open and Fawn burst in. Her eyes were Christmas-morning shiny.

"Mama Hutchie! Will!" she was yelling.

"I'm right here in front of you," Will said. He hoped his voice didn't sound as sour as his mouth suddenly felt.

"Oh," Fawn said. She turned to the man standing behind her, who wasn't a whole lot taller than Will himself, but who had a healthy-looking set of square shoulders and a dark, serious face.

"This is my dad!" Fawn said, and then she promptly hiked herself up onto his back and wrapped her arms around his neck so that her cheek was nestled next to his.

"Isn't he the best?" Fawn said. "Isn't he the tallest—the handsomest—the strongest?"

Fawn's father smiled a slow smile that transformed his somber face into something almost boyish. The skin around his eyes crinkled until the eyes themselves nearly disappeared.

"I'm Dan," he said, and let go of Fawn's legs long enough to shake Will's hand.

Will stood up, knocking the chair sideways and feeling like a dolt. He was glad when Mom swept into the kitchen and took over the conversation.

"Sergeant McHorse," Mom said with her usual ease. "I'm so glad to meet you."

"Call me Dan, please," Fawn's father said. "I'm the one who should be honoring you." He turned his head to look at Fawn, who was still beaming like a lighthouse. "My daughter is a different young lady than she would have been without your care. God bless you."

Young lady? Will thought. *Huh. He hasn't been around her long enough!*

"Well, Conchita," Mom was saying to the woman who was standing behind Fawn and her father. "How does it feel to have your little family together again?"

Why are you even bothering to ask, Mom? Will wanted to say. *She's not gonna answer that—she never talks.*

But Fawn's mother peeked out from behind her Fawn-laden husband and said, "I must always be pinching myself to discover—is it real?"

Will knew his mouth was hanging open, but it was hard not to gape. This wasn't the shy, backward woman they used to call Frog Woman, who a year before couldn't look anyone in the eye and who let Margretta Dietrich do all her talking for her. She looked at Dan with melted eyes now and gave a low, throaty chuckle before she stepped back behind him.

Fawn, on the other hand, was hugging her father's neck so hard, Will thought he was starting to look a little blue.

You're gonna wear him out the first day, Will thought. He looked away so Fawn wouldn't see the envy he knew was smeared all over his face.

"Hop down, chickadee," Dan said. "I need a few minutes to thank Mrs. Hutchinson properly."

"That's no Mrs.," Fawn said as she slid from her father's back. "That's Mama Hutchie."

Mom gave her almost-smile. "But you can call me Ingrid," she said.

He looks like he wants to call her Queen *Ingrid,* Will thought. They were moving dangerously close to getting mushy, and Will was anxious to get out of there. He caught Fawn's eye, at a rare moment when she wasn't gazing up at her father as if he were General Eisenhower himself, and nodded toward the door.

Fawn followed him out to the back stoop, but not before assuring her father that she would be right back. She and Will had no sooner shut the screen door behind them than she said, "Isn't my dad the best, Will? Isn't he the handsomest? Isn't he—"

"Yeah, yeah, he's all that stuff," Will said. "Hey—"

"Hey what?"

Will nodded at the flowered sundress she was wearing. "How are you gonna ride a horse in that?"

"I'm not gonna ride a horse."

"We're supposed to ride Señora Otero's horses every day—we promised."

Fawn looked at him as though he'd suddenly grown an extra nose. "Not now that my dad's home, silly boy!" she said. "I gotta spend time with him!"

"Yesterday you were scared of him," Will said.

"Was not!"

"Were too!"

"Well, I was stupid, then," Fawn said. She set her jaw stubbornly. "He's the best dad in the world."

"Next to mine," Will said.

"Nuh-uh! Mine's the best!"

Will grunted.

"He is, Will Hutchinson!" she said. Her face bent itself into a scowl, and her fists doubled.

"Okay, okay," Will said. "He's the best dad in New Mexico right now."

Fawn seemed to consider that, still frowning. Finally, she let her hands relax and said, "I'll let you off this time."

Although Will only gave her another grunt, he was secretly glad she was letting him off. He didn't feel like peeling her off his back today. Suddenly he didn't feel like doing anything.

Fawn and her parents left shortly after that, and Reverend Bud dropped Abe off so that he and Will could ride bikes out to Mr. T.'s ranch. Since it was Saturday, Abe was out of school, and he was bubbling over at the prospect of spending a whole day with Will and Miguel and Olive—and Fawn.

"Where Fawn?" the big guy said as Will checked his bicycle tires to be sure they had enough air to manage Abe's weight on the back.

"She's not comin' today," Will said. "She's with her dad."

"Horsies?" Abe said.

"Nope. She's with her mom and dad." Will stood up. "I think this'll hold us. Let's go, pal."

But Abe shook his big head of butter-colored hair, his pale eyes drooping with confusion. "Fawn," he said. "Horsies."

Will tried not to sigh too loudly. It wasn't Abe's fault that he was a slow thinker and would probably never be able to operate beyond a second-grade level, even though he towered over Will and weighed twice as much. He'd always tried to be patient when Abe asked the same question 20 times, but today it was hard.

I don't need to keep being reminded that everything's changing, he thought. It seemed to Will that God had suddenly snapped His fingers and the world had rearranged itself. *And I don't care what Mom says,* he told himself as he and Abe wheeled their plodding way down Canyon Road. *I didn't have any choice about it!*

By the time they reached the ranch south of Santa Fe that belonged to the junior high principal, Mr. Tarantino—whom they all called Mr. T.—Will was afraid he was going to scream if Abe asked him one more time: *Fawn? Horsies?* He was glad to turn him over to a smiling Señora Otero, who led him off to the kitchen where she cooked for Mr. T., and where she promised there were some hot sopa-pillas waiting for him. For once Will was glad Abe was still afraid of the horses and wouldn't go riding.

Feeling a little guilty, Will headed for the stable where Olive was already saddling up Hilachas, the horse Miguel usually rode.

"Where's Miguel?" he said.

Olive looked at him over Hilachas's spotted-Appaloosa back. Her dark hair was pulled back at the sides with hairpins, so that her face looked more square than ever. Will never admitted it to anyone, but he liked her face.

"He's playing the guitar at LaFonda Hotel," she said. "The summer crowd is in, so they have work for him again."

"A bunch of women pinching his cheeks," Will said.

Olive raised an eyebrow. "What's eating you?" she said. "Did you get out on the wrong side of the bed this morning?"

"No," Will said. "There's only one side I can get out on."

"Then it's the grumpy side." Olive looked around. "Where's Fawn?"

"She's not comin'," Will said. "Her dad just got back."

"Oh," Olive said. "I get it."

"You get what?" Will said.

"Why you're so grouchy. But don't worry, I'll cheer you up."

She grinned in that matter-of-fact way she had. Will just grunted.

"Now this looks like a happy crew!"

It was Mr. T., striding in on his long legs, his hat shading his tan face and hiding what Will knew was his good-natured smile of bright white teeth. Why did everybody else have to be in such a good mood? It made him feel worse.

"Half of us are happy," Olive said. "Now if the other half would just saddle up his horse—"

She jerked her head toward Cisco, the big workhorse, who was muttering under his breath in his stall.

"You two interested in a little change today?" Mr. T. said.

"I guess," Will said. He headed for the tack room.

Behind him, Mr. T. said to Olive, "Why don't you ride north of town today, just for something new? I think Will could use a change of scenery."

It's gonna take more than that to cheer me up, Will thought.

But Olive was determined—he could tell by the straight way she sat in the saddle on Hilachas and led the way around the dusty outskirts of Santa Fe and into the hills north of town.

She pointed out an elk and a comical roadrunner, but Will only answered in grunts. Riding without Fawn *and* Miguel was making him gloomier than ever. Finally, Olive tried a different approach.

"Mr. T. says I have to start thinking about what courses to take at the high school in the fall," she said. "I haven't been to school in so long, it's kind of exciting."

Will guessed maybe it was, for her. Ever since her mother had died three years ago, Olive had been tutored by her father in the tin shack they'd lived in up in the hills. She hadn't had friends or ball games or homework in all that time, although Will didn't see how anybody could miss homework.

"So what are you taking in eighth grade next year?" Olive said. "I missed junior high completely."

Will shrugged.

"Don't you even care?" she said.

"I guess so," Will said. "But I don't think it matters much what I pick."

Olive turned in the saddle to look at Will over her shoulder. Both eyebrows were raised.

"You have to start thinking about your future," she said. "You're not gonna be a kid in school forever."

"Sure seems like it."

Olive's dark eyes narrowed, and she pulled back on Hilachas's reins. The horse came to a stop in mincing steps.

"Will Hutchinson," she said, "are you feeling sorry for yourself?"

"No," he said. He could feel his lips hanging down in a sulk.

"You have to snap out of it," Olive said.

"And how am I supposed to do that?"

"You can start by—"

Suddenly, Hilachas tossed his head and gave a nervous whinny. Cisco stepped sideways, and Will could feel the horse's muscles tightening.

"Easy," Olive said to her horse. "It's okay."

"No, it's not," Will said. "It's another one of those things, I bet."

"What things?"

As if in answer, in the distance there was a threatening rumble that shook the ground. The leaves on a nearby cottonwood clapped like an anxious audience, and both horses strained in their halters.

"Is it an earthquake?" Olive asked as she struggled to keep Hilachas under control.

"I'm not sure what it is," Will said. "They say it's coming from up there."

He pointed toward Los Alamos, which he knew more than saw was atop the Pajarito Plateau to the north.

"That far away?" Olive said. "It must be something pretty big."

By now her knuckles were white from holding onto the reins, and Will himself was having trouble keeping an agitated Cisco from hightailing it across the desert.

"I'd sure like to know what it is," Will said.

Olive gave him a sly look. "Do you think it matters?" she said.

"Maybe," Will said.

Just then they heard another rumble, closer this time and not as threatening. As it drew louder, Will realized it was a car engine.

Down the road he could see a cloud of dust choking the already dry, hot air.

"Let's get the horses away from that," Olive said.

Will nodded and urged Cisco behind a jumbled pile of rocks. Olive followed on Hilachas and they both dismounted, not a moment before the vehicle roared past.

"That's a funny-looking car," Olive said, peering around the rock pile.

"It's a Jeep!" Will said. "I've seen pictures of 'em in *LIFE* magazine and newsreels and stuff!"

"What's a Jeep?"

"This swell little car with no top—looks like a metal box on wheels. They use 'em in the army."

"Lovely," Olive said dryly.

"It can go anywhere—off the road, over hills. It's like it's science fiction or something."

"It's stopping," Olive said.

Will stood up so he could see over the top of her head. Just before the road took a curve, several hundred yards away, he could see the dust settling around the Jeep, though there was still enough in the air to make it hard to see the figure who climbed out of it.

"What's she doing?" Olive said.

"She?" Will said. "Driving a Jeep?"

"Girls can drive Jeeps!" Olive said.

Will didn't remind her that only moments before she didn't even know what a Jeep was. He squinted through the haze of dust and saw that Olive was right—the figure was wearing a dress. The hot wind whipped at its short hem as she swung open a gate. Will and Olive watched her climb back into the Jeep, drive it through, and then get out and close the gate behind her.

"I think she's locking it," Olive said. "I wish we had a telescope or something so we could see better."

"Why would anybody lock a gate up here?" Will said. "Who's gonna wanna drive up there anyway?"

"Evidently she does," Olive said. "I wonder why she isn't wearing a uniform."

"Huh?"

"You said they use those Jeep things in the army. She doesn't look like she's in the army to me. She has on a recent style—you know, short skirt, not very full—I heard that's because we're supposed to be saving on fabric—"

Will ignored most of that. Dresses didn't excite him. What did excite him was the idea that something mysterious really was going on—and maybe it had something to do with what was happening at Los Alamos.

"Well, finally," Olive said.

"Huh?" Will said.

"Finally you don't look like you already died and forgot to fall down." She grinned her squarish grin. "I don't know what you're thinking, but I'm glad you're thinking it. The old Will is back."

Chapter Three

*W*ill was glad to have something else to think about, and think about it he did, all the way back to Mr. T.'s ranch and all the way home on his bike with Abe in tow. Although Abe was still mumbling behind him about "Fawn and horsies," Will's mind was on ladies in flowered dresses letting themselves into locked gates, behind which mysterious things were obviously happening. There were no answers yet, but at least the questions were better than thoughts of the changes happening in his life that were beyond his control.

I don't even need to think about Fawn, he told himself as he dropped Abe off at home. *I betcha pretty soon, now that I'm working on this with Olive, I'll forget all about her.*

But when he finally got back to his house on Canyon Road, he saw that forgetting was the last thing he was going to be able to do. Greeting him in the kitchen were Margretta Dietrich and Conchita and Dan and, of course, Fawn herself.

"Surprise," Mom said as she pulled a ham out of the oven. "The gang's all here."

"Yeah," Will said. *Swell.*

If anyone noticed that he was gritting his teeth and looking hopefully at all the exits, they didn't say so. As far as Will could tell, they were so wrapped up in each other, they barely noticed he was there. Even when they sat down at the table, the most anybody said to him directly was, "Could you pass the squash?"

The rest of the time, it was Fawn who steered the conversation.

"We had the best day ever," she said, almost before Mom finished asking the blessing. "We went shopping for clothes for Dad. 'Course, I think he should keep on wearing his uniform so everybody knows he's a war hero—"

"I'm not a hero, chickadee," Dan said. "I just did my duty."

"See how brave he is?" Fawn said. "I bet he's the bravest soldier in the whole army—"

Swell, Will thought. *Now he's not only the handsomest and the tallest and the strongest, he's the bravest, too. Brother.*

"And then we talked about the wedding," Fawn babbled on. "Mama and Daddy are gonna have a real church wedding this time—since they didn't have one before because everybody in their families was mad at them for marrying outside the tribe—and today we got this lady to say she'd make Mama's wedding dress out of that parachute Dad sent me."

"You've been a busy group," Margretta said. "What's on your agenda for tomorrow?"

"Only two of the horses got ridden today," Will said. "Tomorrow you oughta—"

"Dad's gonna borrow Reverend Bud's car and we're gonna go to Tesuque," Fawn said.

Big deal, Will thought. *That's only six miles away. It's not like you're going to California or something.*

But it might as well have been Australia, as excited as Fawn was. All during dessert, she babbled on about the picnic lunch they were going to pack and where they were going to eat it. Finally, Will couldn't take any more. When the last person was finished, he jumped up and said, "I'll clear the table."

Isn't there anything else *to talk about?* he thought as he carried a stack of plates into the kitchen and let them clatter to the counter. Once again he looked longingly at the back door and wondered what Mom would do if he just escaped until they'd all gone home. To their little apartment. Where they'd be together—

"I thought I'd give you a hand," said a voice behind him.

Will turned with a jerk to see Dan standing there with his own pile of dishes, and he was sure for a wild moment that Dan had been reading his thoughts. He tried to will the guilty look off of his face and said, "No, that's okay. I can do it."

"Yeah, but I needed an excuse to get out of there," Dan said. "I'm not used to so much female conversation. For the last couple of years, I've been pretty much surrounded by smelly men talking about their cars and their baseball teams."

"But you don't have to help, honest. You're the guest."

"I hope not," Dan said.

He looked at Will from eyes set deeper into his face than most people's. Will found himself wanting to look away, sure that Dan could see his thoughts sparring with each other in his head.

"I don't want to be a guest in this house," he said. "I want to be considered as much a part of the family as Fawn is."

She's not anymore! Will wanted to say. But he nodded and turned on the water to rinse the forks.

Dan picked up a dish and scraped its remains into the trash can. "Now *this* seems strange," he said. "A couple of months ago, I'd have been glad to have this much for dinner. Now I'm dumping it into the garbage." He chuckled. "Boy, it's good to be home—not that it ever felt like home before I went. Funny how things change when you're without everything you took for granted."

Will didn't answer, but he couldn't help listening. Dan had a deep, soft voice that always seemed on the verge of a laugh. If he'd just talk about something else.

"Take Fawn, for instance," Dan went on. "Before I went off in the army, I have to admit I never paid that much attention to her. Frankly, I thought she was kind of a pain in the neck."

"She still is," Will said.

Dan grinned. His eyes did their disappearing act.

"It's a pain I don't ever want to be without again," he said. "I'm so proud of her—did you know she read *Laughing Boy,* the whole thing?"

"Yeah," Will said. "She picked it out—but Mom made her read every night."

"One of hundreds of things I have to be grateful to your mother for. And you, too."

Will shrugged. "I didn't make her read."

"But you've been a good friend to her," Dan said. "She's done nothing but talk about you ever since I got home. Will this and Will that. At first I was a little bit jealous. *I* wanted to be her hero."

"I'm sure not her hero!" Will said, splashing soap over the side of the sink. "If I ever said I was, she'd jump me!"

"She's pretty feisty, isn't she?" Dan said. "That's one thing that hasn't changed. But a lot of other things have—for the better—and I have you to thank for some of that." He wiped his hands on the dishtowel and looked at—into—Will again. "That's why I'd like for you to be my best man at our wedding."

Will stopped, his hands dunked in soapy water, and stared at Dan.

"We don't know each other that well," Dan said, "but I feel like we've been friends forever, as much as Fawn's told me about you. And you've been more of an influence on her than any other man in her life so far, especially when it comes to God being real to her. I want you standing next to me up there at the altar." His voice got deeper and softer. "I found the Lord when I was overseas, but I think there's a lot I could learn about Him from you."

Too many things were competing for attention in Will's head for him to answer—everything from the thought of the neck-squeezing bow tie he would have to wear in the wedding, to the idea that he really had been a big brother to Fawn—and that now her father had come home to take over.

It was enough to make him want to say, *No thanks. I'd rather climb into this sink and bathe in dirty dishwater than be your best man.*

But one thought out-shouted the rest of them—the one that said, *You might as well be his best man. Not doing it isn't going to change anything. No matter what Mom said, this choice isn't gonna matter one way or the other.*

"Sure. I'll do it," he said.

Dan grinned and stuck out his hand.

"Mine are wet," Will said.

"What does that matter between friends?" Dan said.

They shook wet, soapy hands, Dan smiling broadly, Will feeling like a bigger fake than a three-dollar bill.

"It will only be a small wedding," Conchita kept saying over the next week.

But for a simple affair, it seemed to Will that it was taking up an awful lot of everybody's time. Mom seemed to be forever running errands for her on her motorcycle, though what could possibly be required besides a big cake and some punch, Will had no idea.

And Fawn was as unavailable as President Truman. Every time Will mentioned going out to the ranch to ride, she looked at him as if he were asking her to go with him on a little jaunt to Japan and said things like, "I'm helping Margretta make the rice bags, Will—honestly!"

Besides the wedding plans, Mom also had Aunt Hildy Helen's upcoming visit to prepare for. Even without Fawn, Will was glad to escape to the ranch every afternoon, just to get out of polishing all the door handles and cleaning out his closet. Why it could even remotely matter to Aunt Hildy what his closet looked like was beyond him—but he promptly put it out of his mind once he got to the ranch every day.

Olive and sometimes Miguel would be waiting for him, except for the days Miguel was playing his guitar at LaFonda. They would saddle up the horses and head north of town, eager to do a little spying on the mysterious gate where they'd seen the Jeep.

But although they got a little closer to the gate and fence each day, they didn't see the Jeep or the flowered-dress lady.

"Are you sure it wasn't our imagination, Will?" Olive said after the fourth day of tying the horses in the shade and creeping from one rock formation to another like fugitives from justice.

"Yeah, I'm sure," Will said. "We both saw it."

"What will happen when we see her again?" Miguel asked.

"I don't know!" Will said, voice snapping like impatient fingers.

"We could slip in the gate behind her when she drives through,"

Olive said. "You know—hide in the dust." She wrinkled her nose at the dirt road. "Heaven knows there's enough of it to hide half the army."

Will felt his mouth falling open.

"Trying to catch flies?" Olive said dryly.

"What if they *are* hiding an army?" Will said.

"*What?*"

"What if this is where they keep Japanese prisoners of war?"

"You really think—"

"Or spies!"

"Is that why there are guns?" Miguel said.

Olive and Will both blinked at him.

"What guns?" Will said.

Miguel pointed, and Will followed with his eyes. He hadn't noticed it before, but there was another fence inside the one where the gate was. It was taller and sturdier looking, even though it was also made of wire. About every 50 yards there was a makeshift tower, and as Will squinted into the afternoon sun, he could see that Miguel was right. Out of each of the towers poked the barrel of a gun, and he had studied enough magazines and newspapers and books on weapons over the past few years to know that they were machine guns.

"Are those real?" Olive said.

"You bet your boots they are!" Will said. "And whoever put 'em there isn't fooling around."

"So it's *not* just something we've dreamed up," Olive said. "They really could be keeping prisoners of war up here."

"Or spies," Miguel said.

"What do you want to bet they torture Japanese spies?" Will said.

"Or train secret agents." Olive wiggled her eyebrows.

Miguel fiddled with the brim of his hat. "I think we must leave now, *mis amigos*," he said. "This sounds dangerous."

Miguel stood up from behind the rock formation that was hiding them from view from the road and began to edge toward the small stand of trees where they'd tied the horses.

Will was about to start reluctantly after him when he heard a sound from down the hill.

"Is that a car motor?" Olive said.

"We must go!" Miguel said, lowering his voice to a mere hiss.

He started to bolt, but Will caught him by the sleeve.

"Stay down!" he said.

"Shhh!" Olive said.

Will wasn't sure why they were all whispering. The engine that was roaring its way up the road would have covered their voices even if they'd been screaming at the tops of their lungs. The three of them crouched low behind the pile of rocks and held their breaths.

I'll look, Will mouthed to them.

Olive and Miguel nodded.

Flattening himself against the back side of the rocks, Will let his face emerge only enough to get a glimpse of the road. What he saw made him choke on the rising dust.

Although the Jeep engine continued running, the car stopped and the same lady, wearing yet another flowered dress that barely covered her knees, jumped from the driver's seat and walked confidently toward the trees. The prickly cactus and the possibility of rattlesnakes didn't seem to bother her at all. When Will saw where she was going, he gasped.

The lady in the flowered dress was headed straight for their horses.

⁜ ⫸ ⁜

Chapter Four

*B*ehind him, Will could hear Olive squeaking, as if she were barely holding back a cry. Will had to bite down on his lip to keep himself quiet. Miguel just gave him a wild-eyed look.

Maybe she has to go to the bathroom, Will wanted to say to him.

But Will didn't believe that himself. He was too afraid to risk sticking his head out again, so he scanned the rock pile, looking for a small opening. There was one gap, just barely above eye level.

Standing on some smaller rocks at his feet, Will could peer through the crack—and see that the woman was shooting down all his theories. She was well into the trees, extending her hand, and Hilachas was nuzzling his nose right into her palm.

"Does she see the horses?" Olive whispered.

Will nodded.

"Then she's gonna know somebody's here."

Will nodded and looked around for an escape route. Miguel gave him a nudge.

"We have done something wrong, my friend?" he whispered.

Olive and Will looked at each other.

"We're spying on her," Will said.

"May we not look?" Miguel said.

Olive nodded. "He's right, Will. She's not in the military—not in that outfit."

Will pressed his eye to the crack again. The lady had by now taken off her straw sun hat so she could rub her face against Virgy's.

Cisco didn't seem to be afraid of her. Through the crack, Will could see him jockeying for position between Hilachas and Virgy and nudging at the lady. She stroked his mane, and Will rolled his eyes. He could practically hear Cisco purring.

But even as she petted Cisco's forehead, her eyes began to roam, through the trees, across the hills, and straight to the pile of rocks that shielded the kids.

Will pulled away from the crack and flattened his back against the stone. He jerked his head for Miguel and Olive to do the same.

"What?" Olive hissed as she pressed like a pancake to the rock wall.

"She's looking for the riders," he whispered. "Only she doesn't want anybody to *know* she's looking."

"But—"

"Shh!" Will said.

He turned and wriggled up to the crack to squint through. The lady was absently pushing Hilachas's nose away from the pocket of her dress, but her gaze was fixed in the direction of the rocks. With a flick of her wrist, she returned the sun hat to her head and pulled it low over her eyes. But Will could still see her mouth painted bright red with lipstick and set as hard and sharp as a knife blade. Will shivered.

"What's wrong?" Olive whispered behind him. "Let me see."

Will stepped down and let Olive have the rock stepping stool so she could look through the crack. She'd barely gotten into position before she whispered, "Evil woman."

"What?" Will said. "What's she doing?"

"She's going back to her Jeep."

"That is good, yes?" Miguel whispered.

"She's still looking around," Olive said. "She wants to find us bad—but I think she's in a hurry to get somewhere."

Even as Olive said it, the Jeep engine roared to life and Will could hear the spray of stones and dirt as the lady pulled away. The kids fell over each other getting to the other end of the rock pile and watched her get out, open the gate, drive through, and close the gate behind her, just as she'd done before. Only this time, she took one long, roaming look behind her.

As soon as the Jeep was out of sight, Olive coughed, waving Jeep dust away from her face.

"We ought to get the horses and get out of here," she said. "In case she comes back."

"Then—we *have* done something wrong?" Miguel said.

Will shook his head. "It's not that. You didn't see her face, Miguel. That's one mean lady."

"I don't think we should come here anymore," Olive said. She doesn't want any visitors, so who's to say the rest of them don't either." Olive looked at Will. "You know I'm right."

Will twisted his lips, but he had to nod. "One more choice we don't get to make the way we want."

Olive patted his head. "Poor baby," she said.

"Think of this, my friend," Miguel said. "We choose to leave this alone. We choose not to be in danger."

"Yeah, I guess," Will said. But to himself he thought, *I could use a little danger right now. It would be better than feeling like I'm in a box all the time.*

It was so hard to figure out, though he tried as the three of them walked toward the stand of trees where the horses waited.

I've been thinking about God a lot. I've been trying to be good because that's what God wants. I've learned all this stuff and I'm trying to live all of it like Mom and Mr. T. and Reverend Bud tell me to, so how come it doesn't make things better?

"What's the matter with him?" Olive said, pointing to Cisco.

From the stand of trees, Cisco was whinnying like a scolding schoolteacher. Will sighed. *Even the horses boss me around,* he thought. "Yeah, yeah. I'm comin'," he said, and picked up the pace.

"It will be okay, my friend," Miguel said as he hurried to keep up with Will. He flashed his smile—the one that charmed all the women at their luncheons at LaFonda.

But as Will looked at him, the smile rose and fell like a piston, and the hand Miguel put on his arm was shaken off as the earth under them jolted and jerked. Olive screamed and fell against Will, snatching at his sleeve as a roar rolled across the mountains above them.

"Get down!" Will cried.

He flung himself to the ground, pulling Olive down with him and falling on top of Miguel. Beneath the pile they formed, the ground gave one last shiver and was quiet. The only sound was that of the tiny pieces of rock pattering back into place around them.

Will was afraid to look up for fear the mountain was about to topple down on them.

"That was the worst one yet!" Olive said as she untangled herself from Will.

"We know one thing for sure now," Will said. "Whatever's doing that is coming from up here." He sat up and pointed. "Look at that."

Behind them a cloud of smoke was settling over the Pajarito Plateau.

"I think we must go," Miguel said. "The horses are frightened."

For the first time, Will realized that Cisco and Virgy and Hilachas were carrying on in the trees, screaming from their throats. Will scrambled up and started toward them with Olive and Miguel on his heels. All three horses were tossing their heads, jerking on the reins that tethered them to the tree trunks. The booming tremors they'd just heard and felt seemed to have them wild with terror—and, strangely, Cisco most of all.

"I'm comin', boy!" Will shouted as he broke into a run.

That didn't seem to do much to reassure Cisco. Will could see his eyes rolling as he jerked on the leather straps.

"Hold on! It's okay!" Will shouted.

Cisco shook his head as if to say, "It's *not* okay!" and the strap snapped.

"No!" Will cried.

Cisco stepped in place until he realized he was free. Then amid Will's shouts, he lowered his head and tore for the hills, leaving the screaming children in a frenzied flurry of dust.

"Cisco, no!" Will shouted again.

He got nothing but a mouthful of flying dirt and a poke from behind from Olive.

"Get on Virgy with me!" she said. "We have to go after him!"

Miguel was already astride Hilachas, digging in his heels and spurring him on. Will hoisted himself up onto Virgy behind Olive, who barely waited for him to get his leg over before she kicked the mare into a gallop.

Will stretched his neck up to look over Olive's mane of hair and blinked against the dust.

"Can you see him?" he shouted.

"All I can see is everything he's kicking up! Close your mouth or you'll choke to death!"

Clamping his lips together, Will held on as they barreled through the cloud Cisco was leaving in his wake. He had no idea how they were going to stop the horse if they did catch up with him.

Behind him, he could hear Hilachas's hooves pounding the ground as Miguel gained on them.

"Slower, Olive!" Miguel shouted.

"What's he saying?" Olive said over her shoulder.

"He says slow down!"

"Why?"

"How should I know?"

Olive pulled back on the reins, but only slightly. It was enough for Miguel to pull Hilachas up beside them.

"I will get ahead of him and cut him off!" Miguel shouted. "You stay behind and we will put him in a box!"

"Put him in a box?" Olive said as Miguel took the lead. "What's he talking about?"

"He means box him in, I think," Will said.

Olive nodded and pulled back more firmly on the reins. Although Virgy stubbornly tossed her head, she slowed down. Miguel was by now flattened completely down onto Hilachas's neck, passing Cisco and getting into position right in front of him. The minute Hilachas began to step in place several yards in front of Cisco, the big horse stopped. Miguel danced Hilachas sideways and reached out his hand.

At once, Cisco seemed to be less frantic. As Olive and Will rode up, Will could see Miguel talking to him and Cisco shaking his head at Miguel, almost as if he were arguing with him.

As Olive and Will rode up behind Cisco, boxing him in, Miguel continued to speak to the big horse in Spanish.

"Do you know what he's saying?" Will said to Olive.

"He's telling him there's double oats waiting for him back at the ranch if he'll just calm down."

"You don't think he really understands him, do you?" Will said.

"Sure looks like it to me."

Cisco did seem to be on his final whinny-protest, and he was still enough for Miguel to get hold of his reins and pull him in. The moment he was close to Hilachas's side, Cisco gave one last snort and settled down like an obedient child.

Although Cisco had stopped breathing hard by the time Miguel had retied the strap and told Will he could get back on, Will said, "Are you sure?"

"You are his master," Miguel said. "Do not show him the fear, and he will trust you."

Feeling like something less than a master of anything, Will slid off of Virgy and stepped gingerly into Cisco's stirrup, hoisting himself over. Cisco whinnied nervously, but Miguel patted his nose and he grew calm.

"He will be fine now," Miguel said.

"Fine or not, we'd better get going," Olive said.

She pointed to the west. Dark clouds had gathered like disgruntled old men and were scowling down on the high desert.

"It's going to be a bad one—lightning and everything," Olive said. "We'd better get home or we're going to hear worse noise than that. I can hear the yelling now."

"Mr. T. doesn't yell," Will said. "And neither does my mom or

Señora Otero." He grunted. "They might send us to our rooms for the rest of our lives—"

By the time they reached the road and picked up speed for the trip home, the storm was rolling in earnest down from the Jemez Mountains to the west and would soon be hitting the very valley they were headed for. The clouds were a threatening black, and lightning bolts were already zigzagging their way down the sky in jagged flashes. Around the horses' feet, the gravelly sand blew, and the clumps of buffalo grass shivered in the wind.

Will reached down to stroke Cisco's mane. "It's just a storm, big fella," he said. "Don't get your tail tangled over it."

He grunted to himself. Somehow it didn't sound the same as when Miguel did it.

Up ahead, Olive spurred Virgy on to go even faster, and Miguel and Will did the same with Hilachas and Cisco. But when the first clap of thunder cracked, Will knew all the speed they could muster wasn't going to put them ahead of what was about to hit them.

Olive pointed to the remains of an adobe building off to their left, and Miguel nodded. It was all Will could do to keep Cisco from taking off like he was in the Kentucky Derby as a lightning bolt cut its way into the dark sky just above them. The thunder crashed within seconds.

"Come on, boy," Will shouted to Cisco. "Let's get to shelter!"

He knew he sounded anything but comforting. There was no point in soothing whispers, though. The wind snatched up every word and hurled it away.

There was no roof on the adobe remains, and there were only two whole walls. The kids guided the horses into the corner they formed.

"Shouldn't we stand between them and the outside?" Will shouted to Miguel over the wind.

Miguel shook his head. "That is too dangerous," he said. "They may try to escape and could knock us down when the next thunder comes."

"We definitely don't want that!" Olive said. "What do we do?"

"Hold the bridle and keep them calm," Miguel said. "But if they try to run, let them go."

Will knew that was the right thing to do, but the image of the three horses tearing off into the mountains wasn't a good one. *We probably* would *hear some yelling if that happened,* he thought.

Virgy settled down, but Cisco flared his nostrils and breathed out protests. Hilachas nudged Miguel's pockets for treats.

"How can you think about food at a time like this?" Olive said to the horse. "All I can think about is how wet we're about to get."

Seconds later, the first big, thick drops of rain came down like warnings of things to come—and then come it did. The wind suddenly kicked up, swirling rain around them and soaking it into their clothes. Will pulled his hat down over his eyes and watched the water pour off the brim like rain out of a gutter.

"It never lasts long!" he shouted over the din.

"It's lasting long enough!" Olive shouted back. "I'm getting soaked to the skin!"

Her hair was already drenched, and it hung in long, drippy panels on either side of her face. Miguel's was dry under his hat, but his shirt was plastered to his body like a second skin.

"You two look like drowned cats!" Will said.

"Oh, and you're ready for the cover of the *Saturday Evening Post* yourself," Olive said.

Will looked down at his dungarees, which were so soaked they had already grown heavy and were making their way off of his waist and down to his hipbones. Water gushed from the cuffs at his ankles.

"Look out," Olive said. "You're about to lose those!"

Miguel put his hand over his mouth, but Olive made no attempt to hide her own glee. She threw back her head and laughed, rain pouring into her open mouth.

"What's so funny?" Will said—but he couldn't help laughing himself. If he looked half as ridiculous as the two of them did, he was ready for a road show.

Miguel let out one of his Spanish whoops that sounded like there were squirrels in his mouth, and Will clamped his arms across his middle to double over. Halfway down he caught sight of something. He straightened up.

Standing where the third wall should have been was a man in uniform. Pointing a gun.

☩ ⸱☦⸱ ☩

Chapter Five

*F*or a fleeting, crazy moment, Will thought the man was a statue. In spite of the storm pelting him from above, he stood perfectly still, except for the slight ripple of his green uniform in the wind and the drip of rain from his helmet. Even that looked orderly.

The helmet itself covered half his face, so that the only thing on it that Will could see was his mouth. When it opened, Will jumped, knocking against Olive and setting Cisco to whinnying under his breath.

"Who are you?" the soldier said. "What are you doing up here?"

Will looked quickly at Miguel. As honest as the kid was, he was sure to blurt out, *I am Miguel Otero and my friends and I were spying on Los Alamos, but we meant no harm!*

Will stepped forward. "We were just up here riding our horses and we had to get out of the rain. Are we on your property?"

"This is government property," the soldier said.

"I'm a little concerned about our government, then," Olive said. "You sure aren't keeping the place up."

Will jerked his head around to look at her. Olive didn't look the least bit concerned.

"It's government property," the soldier said again, mechanically.

It made Will wonder if that was the only answer he knew.

"Well, excuse us," Olive said. "As soon as it stops raining, we'll be on our way."

For the first time, the soldier moved something besides his mouth. He motioned behind him with the side of the gun. "Let's go," he said.

"Go where?" Olive said. "We haven't done anything wrong."

"This is government property—"

"We got that part! But we didn't know it, and as soon as it stops raining we'll leave."

"We are wet anyway," Miguel said. "Perhaps we should leave now."

"Sounds like a good plan to me!" Will said.

He turned to take hold of Cisco's bridle.

"Halt!" the soldier said. "Don't make another move."

"Señor, if you please," Miguel started to say.

Obviously, the soldier wasn't as easily charmed as the ladies at LaFonda.

"That's enough!" he said. "Let's go, all three of you."

"We can't leave our horses," Will said. "We'll ride straight out of here, right back to Santa Fe—we promise."

"We will not look back, sir," Miguel said.

Will gave Olive a hard look.

Don't say anything, he said to her with his eyes. *Let's just get outa here!*

"All right, mount up," the soldier said. "I'm going to watch you go. Anybody so much as turns around—"

"And you'll do what—shoot us down?" Olive said. "Innocent children? Oh, please."

She rolled her eyes. Will groaned inwardly.

Both of them froze when a loud click came from the gun. The soldier had it positioned at his shoulder, the barrel toward them. "I will do what I have to," he said. This time Olive only stared at the gun. Miguel was already halfway into his saddle.

"You don't have to shoot us," Will said. "We're leaving."

"And you won't be coming back—am I right about that?"

"Yes," Will said.

He gave Olive a poke, which got her scurrying to Virgy. When they were both in their saddles, the soldier lowered the gun and motioned them out of their adobe corner. Miguel nodded for Olive to go first, which she did, with her nose in the air in spite of the rain. Miguel barely looked up as he followed, his body bent like a whipped dog.

Will wasn't sure what to do, so he nodded at the soldier as he passed him. The man made a sound which for an instant sounded like a caught-back laugh. But when Will turned his head to see, the gun came up and waved him on.

"Don't so much as look back," the soldier said. "You've seen the last of this place."

The rain was slowing to its last few drops, but Will hardly noticed as he clicked his tongue at Cisco and they trotted off after Miguel and Olive. Miguel was riding as if the entire army were after him. Olive was going none too slowly on Virgy, though Will could tell from the way she was sitting in the saddle that she was trying to pretend she wasn't in a hurry. Will dug his heels into Cisco and caught up with them.

"Is he still back there watching us?" Olive said.

"I don't know," Will said. "I don't have eyes in the back of my head."

"He said we must not look back," Miguel said.

"He's not the boss of us," Olive said. "He can't tell us what to look at and what not to look at."

"Then why don't you look?" Will said.

As soon as the words crossed his lips, he wanted to snatch them back, but it was too late. Olive whipped her head around. An instant later, there was a sharp crack.

"He is shooting at us!" Miguel cried.

He didn't wait for anyone to hold him back. His feet came out and he slammed them into Hilachas's sides. The horse took off like a shot past Olive, and Cisco strained against the reins to be off after him.

"We'd better get him before he hurts himself," Olive said.

Will didn't remind her that Miguel had grown up with these horses and knew them better than almost anybody. He was just happy to put as much distance between himself and the gun-carrying soldier as he could.

"What did he take off like that for?" Olive shouted from behind him as they both took out after Miguel.

"Uh—because we were being shot at!"

"He shot in the air," Olive said. "He was just trying to scare us."

"It worked! Does everybody up there take mean pills or something?"

"That guy was faking it," Olive said. "When I looked back, he was laughing at us."

Will would have argued with her, except that he'd thought he'd heard laughter in the soldier's voice himself. He looked out ahead, where Miguel was disappearing down into the valley, kicking up a screen of mud behind him.

We're never gonna convince Miguel of that, he thought. *If Olive and I are ever gonna come back up here, we're gonna have to do it without him.*

They finally got back to the ranch, hair hanging in strings from their heads, clothes still wringing wet. Will thought they must have been pretty comical to look at, but Mr. T. and Señora Otero looked anything but amused when they greeted them in front of the stables.

Mr. T. glanced up at the sky, which was quickly growing dark. "Are you kids all right?" he said.

Both Will and Olive looked at Miguel. He seemed to feel their message, because he said, "We're fine."

"Good," Mr. T. said, "then let's get down to brass tacks."

They followed him inside.

"Shouldn't we take care of the horses first?" Will said. He avoided Mr. T.'s eyes.

"This isn't going to take that long," Mr. T. said. There was none of the usual mirth as he squinted at each of them in turn. "Is there some reason why you stayed out when you saw a storm coming in— and didn't get yourselves back here until nearly dark?"

"No!" Will and Olive said together.

Miguel put in a weaker version.

"We were worried," Señora Otero said. "Very worried."

Will couldn't look at her, either. There was sure to be disappointment in her eyes, and he didn't want to see that. He had always wanted Miguel's beautiful, soft-spoken mother to think the best of him.

But *nobody* seemed to be thinking the best of them at the moment. Gabby, one of Mr. T.'s ranch hands, clattered past them in his boots, muttering under his breath as he eyed the wet horses.

Will swallowed hard. "We're sorry, Mr. T.," he said. "It won't happen again."

"No, I'm sure it won't," Mr. T. said, "because from now on, you will not be allowed to ride the horses unless there is an adult with you."

Olive opened her mouth. Mr. T. shut it with a look. He hadn't been a principal for all those years without learning something.

"There will be no discussion about this," he said. "These are Señora Otero's horses, and as long as you are taking them from my property I am responsible for anything that happens to you. This is up to us to decide, and we have decided. That's the end of it."

He swept his eyes over the three of them. No one spoke a word, not even Olive.

"As soon as you're finished with the horses," he said to Will, "you'd better get on home before your mother starts worrying as well."

He and Señora Otero turned toward the door. Beside Will, Miguel gave a sigh that seemed to come from his toenails. Will glanced down at him. He was looking after his mother, pain etched into his face. Will felt like a heel.

"Señora?" Will said. "It wasn't Miguel's fault, us staying gone so long. It was our idea—Olive's and mine. He shouldn't get punished like us."

"I said the discussion was over," Mr. T. said. "What is it about that you don't understand, Will?"

Señora Otero put her hand on Will's arm. "Miguel makes his own choices," she said. "And he must take his own consequences."

There was silence until the adults' footsteps faded across the yard. Then Will gave his loudest grunt yet.

"What?" Olive said.

"Choices," Will said. "I don't see any choices, do you?"

"We choose to obey or not to obey," Miguel said. His voice was quiet, but not warm. Will could feel a chill around him.

"That's not much of a choice if you ask me," Will said.

"It doesn't look like anybody's asking you, does it?" Olive said.

They didn't talk again as they unsaddled the horses and brushed them down and covered them with blankets against the night chill. They muttered good-byes when Olive walked off toward the guest cottage where she stayed with Señora Otero, and Miguel went into the house.

The only thing good about Will's ride back to Santa Fe was that it dried out his clothes. For the most part, it was long and lonely. The sky was a velvety navy blue after the rain, but he wasn't in the mood for beauty. He was in the mood to get up to his room so he could scream frustration into his pillow.

But when he leaned his bike against the garage behind the house, Will heard voices coming from the kitchen.

Aw, man, company tonight? Will thought.

Setting his jaw for the argument he was sure was about to take place, Will marched resolutely up the back steps and pulled open the screen door.

Mom looked up at him, beaming. Across the table from her was a dark-haired woman with huge eyes. She seemed vaguely familiar, but she didn't look as if she recognized Will at all.

"You remember your Aunt Hildy Helen," Mom said. "Surprise— she got in a day early."

That wasn't the real surprise, as far as Will was concerned. The real surprise was that she wasn't at all the way Will remembered her in those misty memories. This woman didn't have the Hutchinson sparkle in her eyes, and she sure didn't look capable of rolling his father down a hill in a barrel or stuffing 10 pieces of bubblegum in her mouth to win a contest. She looked pale and thin and completely without a sense of humor.

"Hi, Will," she said in a flat voice. "You've grown tall."

Will shrugged. "Yeah, well, people don't grow shorter, do they?"

She didn't smile.

"That's what Uncle Al always says to me," he said quickly. "I guess I got being a smart aleck from him."

She showed no sign of agreeing—or disagreeing, for that matter.

"Aunt Hildy thought she was going to be at Bruns the whole day, but they let her go after a quick checkup," Mom said.

Will looked at her blankly. He had no idea what she was talking about.

"Bruns," Mom said. "The army hospital—you know."

"Oh, yeah," Will said. He turned to Aunt Hildy. "Did you get shot or something?"

Aunt Hildy shook her head.

"A bomb?" Will said.

"Do I hear a car coming up the drive?" Mom said. She walked over to the window. "It's Bud," she said. She turned to Aunt Hildy. "He's the assistant pastor at our church. I'm anxious for you to meet him."

Aunt Hildy didn't look anxious to meet him, or anybody else. She folded her hands on the table and stared at them.

I bet she was a lot of fun in those clubs overseas, Will thought. *Morale must be at an all-time high with her around.*

"Knock knock!" Bud called in through the screen door.

Although Bud pushed it open and came on in as he always did, Will rushed toward him. He hoped Bud could see the message "*Get me out of here!*" in his eyes.

Introductions were made, and Aunt Hildy seemed even less

enthused about meeting Reverend Bud than she had been about seeing Will. The more she withdrew, the harder Mom fought to make everything bright and cheery. Will got tired just watching her.

"Sit down, Bud," she said. "I don't have a thing to offer you except a glass of ice water. I was going to do my baking tomorrow, but Hildy Helen sneaked up on me tonight!"

"That's all right, Ingrid," Reverend Bud said. "I really came to steal Will away for an hour or so. We haven't had a chance to spend any time together since Tina and I got back from Washington."

Will turned to his mother in case begging became necessary, but she was already nodding.

"Bud has been so wonderful to Will," she said to Aunt Hildy. "He's like a substitute dad. I know Rudy's going to be so pleased—"

"Excuse me," Hildy Helen said.

She pushed herself away from the table with a scrape of the chair on the tile floor and rushed out of the room.

"What was *that* all about?" Will said.

Mom put her finger to her lips.

"Everything all right?" Bud said.

Evidently not, Will thought. *We have a crazy woman living in our house!*

"I think it will be," Mom said. "But it's going to take some time. Why don't you two go ahead and go out. I don't think she's up for company tonight."

Will couldn't get out the back door fast enough.

✛ ⚜ ✛

Chapter Six

*I*t's such a nice night," Bud said as they went down the back steps together. "What do you say we walk to the Plaza Café and have a malt?"

"I'd walk all the way to Albuquerque to get out of there," Will said, nodding toward the house.

Bud shook his head. "Your mother said your aunt was ill, but I didn't realize how bad it was. It's a shame."

Will thought the real shame was that Aunt Hildy appeared to have lost her entire personality overseas.

As they crossed the Castillo Bridge over what was in the summer the mere trickle of the Santa Fe River, Bud filled him in on the happenings at the Kateses' house.

"I thought we were happy having Abe with us before," he said. "But now that the adoption is final and he's officially ours, we feel more like a family than ever. It's what Tina and I have always wanted."

"I don't think he remembers any parents but you," Will said.

Bud gave his Elmer Fudd laugh—the one Will had at one time thought was goofy, but which he now knew was just Bud.

"That's the beauty of Abe," Bud said. "People say, 'But you're going to have to take care of him all his life,' and I say, 'That's right. Other people have to let their kids go when they grow up. We get to keep ours forever.'"

By now they'd crossed Alameda to Cathedral Place and were moving in the direction of the LaFonda Hotel, where the mariachis were playing loudly enough to be heard all the way to Los Alamos. Even from a block away, Will could see that other people were out enjoying the velvety summer night. There were tables on the patio near the sidewalk, filled with chattering folks sipping icy drinks.

"That looks like Agent Graves," Bud said as they drew nearer.

He motioned to a man with a pipe who sat alone in a rustic leather chair, gazing about him from under his straw, snap-brim hat. In his gray suit, he looked out of place among the Hispanics with their costumes that flashed color as they endlessly moved.

But no one else seemed to notice him. Will knew that probably the only reason Bud did was because Agent Graves of the FBI had once helped him and the Hutchinsons when they wanted to enroll their Japanese friends, the Lins, in Santa Fe's public schools and some citizens had protested.

Since then, Will hadn't thought much about the agent, though he always seemed to be around, puffing on his pipe and watching people. But an idea struck Will as he and Bud took one of the four paths that crossed the grassy Plaza.

I never could figure out what he does in Santa Fe—but what if it has something to do with what's going on up at Los Alamos? What if they are keeping captured spies up there? Then it would make sense that the FBI would be part of it. Huh.

Bud nudged him with his elbow as he opened the door to the Plaza Café and motioned Will inside. "You *must* have something on your mind," he said. "I just offered you a banana split instead of a malt, and all you did was grunt."

"Oh—sorry," Will said. He grinned at Bud. "Is the offer still open?"

"Only if you tell me where your mind keeps wandering off to."

Will really had no problem telling Bud. He'd learned a long time ago that Bud was a person he could trust with anything from his bad moods to the daydreams that made a lot of other people give him the isn't-that-cute look.

As they climbed onto the chrome stools at the counter and looked up at the specials, he wondered why he hadn't thought about asking Bud about Los Alamos before. Will wasn't the only person who trusted Bud. Bud talked to a lot of people—maybe even Los Alamos people.

"I'm kinda curious about what's going on up at Los Alamos," Will said.

"Who isn't?" Bud said.

"Did you know they have barbed wire fences about 10 feet tall? And they're miles out from the hill—"

Bud looked so quickly from the menu to Will, his chubby cheeks jiggled. He puckered his eyebrows.

"You've been up there?" he said.

"Yeah—Miguel and Olive and me. We saw the machine guns and everything. And this one soldier—"

"Will, don't go up there again."

Will stared. There was no longer anything jolly about Bud's face. His eyes had taken on a sharpness Will had never seen in them before.

"We can't anyway," Will said. "We got back late, so Mr. T. and Señora Otero won't let us ride without an adult anymore. Besides, we got chased off by—"

"That's good. Now, you stay away. It's not a place for you kids to be hanging around—or anybody else, for that matter."

"Then you do know something about it," Will said.

"Two banana splits," Bud said to the lady behind the counter. "Double whipped cream for my friend here."

Will leaned toward him. "What's going on up there? Do you know?"

"I probably don't know any more than you do. I just know that it's dangerous. You said yourself, they have machine gun emplacements."

"Uh-huh—and soldiers with guns that point them at kids."

Bud's pudgy face darkened. "Someone pointed a gun at you?"

"Yeah. He only shot it in the air, but—"

"Will, I want you to make me a promise."

Will had to nod.

"Promise me that you will not go anywhere near that place again. Do your riding south of town or something, but stay away from Los Alamos."

"But why—"

"You kids are like my own. If anything happened to any of you, it would be like losing Abe. I'd never be the same."

"Yeah, but how do you know something might happen to us? I mean, why do they have soldiers with guns up there in the first place?"

"There's still a war on, Will," Bud said. "And there are things about it that we civilians just need to keep out of."

Will opened his mouth to protest, but Bud turned his full focus on the two banana splits that were sliding toward them across the counter.

"Would you get a load of this?" he said. "Look at me—my mouth's watering."

Will look glumly at his sundae.

"Not enough whipped cream?" Bud said.

"Nah, it's fine."

"But *you're* not fine."

Will shook his head and poked at the ice cream with the tip of his spoon. "I'm just sick of not having any say in anything that happens to me. And don't tell me I just need to keep praying, because I've *been* praying."

"Oh, I know that," Bud said. "I've seen a big change in you, just in the past few months.

"Then how come everything's all messed up?"

"Give me some examples," Bud said. He motioned toward Will's banana split with his spoon. "And eat that before it melts. I hate to see a perfectly good serving of something incredibly fattening go to waste."

But Will just toyed with his spoon. "It's like this," he said. "There are all these things I wanna change. Like I want my dad home. And I wanna be a family like you and Abe and Tina are and Fawn and her mom and dad. And I want Olive to have any kind of family at all."

"And you're praying about all of that."

"Yeah, but then there are some things that I *don't* want to change—only they keep changing anyway."

"Such as?"

"Fawn not living with us anymore. Fawn not even hanging around with us anymore because she spends every minute with her father. Us not being allowed to ride the horses by ourselves now." He gave the split a stab and dropped the spoon on the counter with a clatter. "It always seems like every time something gets good, something comes along to change it, and I can't do anything about it. It's just like when me and Kenichi got to be best friends, he up and moved to Albuquerque. Then Miguel's my best friend—and he moves out to the ranch. I still get to see him almost every day, but it's not the same as him bein' in town. Next thing you know, Olive'll be moving to Timbuktu and I'll never see her again. Mom talks about me making the right choices, but I don't think my choices matter—so what's the point?"

Bud made a soft noise in his throat. Will looked up to see him nodding.

"I get what you mean," he said. He tapped his spoon on the edge of Will's dish. "Do you mind?" he said.

Will shook his head, and Bud dipped into Will's melting split and chewed thoughtfully. His own dish was already empty.

"I think I have a solution for you," he said finally.

"You're gonna say to pray, aren't you?" Will said. "I already told you, I *am* praying."

"This goes beyond just praying—do you want the rest of this?"

Will pushed the dish toward him, shaking his head. Bud polished off the split, wiped his lips with his napkin, and leaned comfortably on the counter. His dark mood was gone.

"Concentrate on the choices that you do have," he said.

"I don't have any."

"Bilgewater! You can choose to be happy for Fawn, or resent her because she has something you wish you had." Bud pulled his eyebrows together again. "You can choose to take my advice when I tell you to stay away from Los Alamos, or you can pursue that and get yourself into trouble."

"That's not really a choice," Will said. "Who wants to get in trouble?"

"You've chosen to see it that way. Some people wouldn't—they'd go ahead and do it anyway."

Will felt his own brows puckering. "No offense, but this isn't helping me."

"That's because I'm not finished yet," Bud said. "Next time you have a choice to make—and you will, trust me—pray that Jesus will show you what choice *He* would make in that same situation."

"And He's gonna show me," Will said. He could hear the doubt weighing down his voice.

"He is. It might be through some example He's given in the Bible, or through some wise person giving you advice—"

"Like you telling me to stay away from Los Alamos."

Bud grinned. "Something like that. And then—and this is the important part—you take action on that. You do what Jesus would do. You can't lose."

"But that's *if* I get any choices," Will said. "The kind of choices I get don't really matter—you know, like whether I ate that banana split or gave it to you."

But patted his stomach. "It sure mattered to me."

"But it doesn't *really* matter—not like a choice that would help my dad come home."

"If you do well with the small choices," Bud said, "God will trust you with bigger ones."

Will could feel his eyes narrowing. "Is that really true? I mean— did it work that way for you?"

"It worked exactly that way. I went from choosing whether to study in school and deciding which girl to ask out, to choosing to accept God's call to be a minister and picking Tina to be my wife." Bud picked up his spoon and scraped his dish for the last traces of ice cream. "Making my choices the way I saw Jesus showing me has made it easier for me to accept the choices I don't have."

"Like not having kids," Will said.

"Exactly. We had no choice in the matter. Tina and I weren't able to have a baby of our own, and we had to accept that. And even choosing to accept instead of being bitter paid off in the long run."

"Because you have Abe."

"Abe, the eternal kid. It's the same with my not being eligible for the draft because of my health. I wanted to serve my country like every other man in this war, but I didn't have that choice. But because I *did* have the choice to come to Santa Fe and I took it, it's been easier for me not to be overseas. I've had important battles to fight right here."

Will didn't answer. It was a lot to take in—bigger than a banana split. Bigger than two.

"You sure you don't want something else?" Bud said. He grinned his pudgy-lipped grin. "It's your choice."

Will said no, and the two of them walked back out into the evening. It was beginning to take on its usual nighttime chill, and Will buttoned his dungaree jacket over his chest as they walked.

The crowd near the Plaza had thinned out by then, and the only sounds were the chattering of the cottonwood leaves as they blew against each other in the breeze and the sleepy warbling of the pigeons.

The long, low Palace of the Governors, which bordered the Plaza on the north with its rough-hewn portal, was silent now that all the women from the Indian pueblos had vacated their daily spots. It always seemed strange to Will to be able to walk freely under the overhang at night, where during the day he had to dodge the displays of blankets and jewelry and pottery and belts, and the shoppers who stopped to dicker over them.

When Will and Bud crossed Washington Street, the noise picked up again. Laughter and radio music floated out of the tiny USO club where off-duty military personnel gathered to take their minds off the war.

Will had always wondered what they did in there and was setting himself up to take a peek when he heard Bud mutter something.

"Looks like the Project moved to another location," he said—more to himself than to Will. He was looking at the door of what appeared to be an empty office.

"What Project?" Will said.

"The Manhattan—"

Bud suddenly stopped.

"Manhattan Project?" Will said. "What's that?"

"I don't know," Bud said. "I just remember that's what they called this."

He turned his face away, appearing to be interested in the lettering on the window of the attorney's place next door—but not before Will caught his expression. His face was the picture of a little boy who has just been caught telling a whopper.

"I'm getting a little chilly," Bud said. "What do you say we head on back to your house?"

"Sure," Will said.

He followed Bud back toward the Plaza and past the sleeping brown earthen buildings that bordered it on the east. He didn't point out that Bud had just made a choice he wasn't sure Jesus would have made.

I mean, come on, he thought. *Jesus didn't lie.*

Will was still musing about the fact that Bud very obviously knew what the—what had he called it?—Manhattan Project was. But why would he say he didn't? And if it weren't important, why would he even notice that their office had moved?

He was so lost in thought—uninterrupted by Bud, who was evidently doing some deep thinking of his own—that they were at the Castillo Bridge before he knew it. The walkway was narrow, and Will let Bud go in front of him. As they walked single file, something below caught Will's eye.

An animal drinking from the river? he thought. *What river? It'd have more luck in a mud puddle.*

He kept walking behind Bud, but he looked back as he went. What he saw made him catch his breath. It wasn't an animal.

Coming out from under the bridge was a man wearing a snap-brim hat. It was Agent Graves.

☩ ☩ ☩

Chapter Seven

*B*ud!" Will whispered.

Bud didn't seem to hear. Will looked back over his shoulder, but Agent Graves was gone.

Did I really see him? Will wondered. He grunted. *Or did I just choose to see him?*

He decided not to mention it to Bud after all. He would probably only tell him not to push his nose into government business.

His mother and Aunt Hildy Helen had already gone to their rooms when Bud dropped him off. Will told Mom good night through her bedroom door and went upstairs to his own room. He stopped in the doorway and looked wistfully down the hall to the room where his aunt was sleeping—where Fawn had slept for so long.

I wish she was still there, he thought as he flopped down on his bed with his clothes still on. *At least I could tell her about the Manhattan Project and Agent Graves. Even if we couldn't do anything about it, I could at least have somebody to tell.*

Above his head, his model airplanes danced on their strings in the breeze that came through his open window.

God? he prayed. *Bud says to pray when I have a choice to make so You—so Jesus—can tell me what to do. But I don't even think I* have *any choices. Maybe I oughta start there, huh? Could You give me a choice about something? Please?*

He was about to go on to suggest a few to God when something hit the screen on his window. It had to be some misguided bird. He turned on his side and closed his eyes again when something else hit like a spattering of gravel.

Will sat up and crawled across the bed to the window. There *were* a couple of pebbles caught in the screen mesh. He undid the catch and pushed the screen out on its hinges. Just as his head emerged, he took a faceful of dirt.

"What the heck?" he said.

"Will?" said a voice from below. "Could you meet me on the back stoop?"

Knocking rocky soil off of his cheeks, Will peered down into the darkness. It was Fawn. He couldn't see her face clearly, but from the way her shoulders were slumped, and the way she was rubbing her hands up and down the sides of her legs, he could tell it wasn't adventure that she had on her mind.

"Yeah," he said to her in a hoarse whisper. "I'll be right there."

Being careful not to make a sound as he crept down the stairs, Will made his way to the back door, mind racing.

I bet it's just what she was afraid of, he thought. *Her dad got drunk and her mom's throwing things at him.*

He tried not to imagine Fawn moving back in with them—somehow that seemed kind of selfish. But if things had gone back to the way they were at her house—

When he pushed open the screen door, Fawn was already sitting on the back steps, her legs pulled up to her chest, her chin resting on her knees as she hugged herself. Now he could see her face in the yellow beams of the porch light. The smile that usually took up its entire lower half had dropped at the corners. She was a miserable sight.

"What's wrong?" Will said. He dropped down onto the step beside her.

"Everything," Fawn said. Even her voice was droopy.

"Are they fighting again?"

"Who?"

"Your parents."

Fawn lifted her chin enough to give him a black look. "No!" she said.

"Then 'everything' isn't wrong," Will said.

"There's enough that's wrong!"

"Like what?"

Fawn looked miserably at her toes, which stuck, naked, out from under the legs of her red-and-white-striped pajamas. "Like—you."

"What did I do?" Will said. "I haven't even been around you!"

"I know. That's what's wrong."

Will rolled his eyes. There was absolutely no understanding girls.

"I don't ever get to see you now—or Olive or Miguel or Abe or Mama Hutchie or—"

"I get the picture," Will said, before she could list everyone in Santa Fe. "But that's not exactly our fault. You're the one who's off with your dad all the time." He put up his hand before she could shoot another one of her looks at him. "But that's okay—I mean, I get it. I'd probably do the same thing—I *will* probably do the same thing when my dad gets home."

"It's not just that," Fawn said. "We went to Tesuque today."

"Yeah," Will said. "Did something go wrong on your picnic? Too many flies? Bad deviled eggs?"

"No."

Will blinked. "Then what's the problem?"

"My dad wants us to move there after the wedding!"

"Oh," Will said.

He opened his mouth to say it was only six miles away, that they would still see each other a lot. But he closed it immediately.

For one thing, I hardly see her now and she's right up the street, he thought. *And I already know how it is with Miguel. Once one thing changes, everything's different.*

"Yeah," he said instead. "I hate it too."

"I don't even get to have any say in it," Fawn said. "My father has it all figured out, and my mother is just gonna go along with it, because I guess that's what wives do." She doubled her fists. "I'm never gonna be a wife if that's what you have to do."

"So you don't get to choose," Will said.

"That's right. And it makes me mad, only I don't wanna be mad at my dad—he just got here!"

Will opened his mouth again, this time to agree with her, when Bud's words whispered in his head. *Next time you have a choice to make pray that Jesus will show you what choice He would make in that same situation.*

"I wonder what Jesus would do if His parents were making Him move," Will said.

"Huh?" Fawn said. She wrinkled her nose at him. "What does Jesus have to do with it?"

Will shrugged. "I'm not sure. But Bud says Jesus has to do with everything."

"Do you know this for a fact?" Fawn said.

"No," Will said. "But I told Bud I'd try it."

"So how do we know what Jesus would do? Nobody ever told *Him* what to do—He was God!"

"They did when He was a kid. They dragged Him all the way to Jerusalem—"

Will stopped. Fawn shoved her knee against his. "So go on," she said.

"They took Him to Jerusalem, remember, when He was 12? He decided to hang around for a while after they left."

"Yeah, but He didn't get in trouble, 'cause His parents knew He was the Son of God."

"He did too get in trouble. They yelled at Him when they found Him."

"Yeah, and then He went back home with them, so He still didn't have any choice." Fawn scowled. "I don't see what this has to do with me. What am I supposed to do, just tell my father that I'm staying here?"

Will considered that. It had sure worked for Bud, listening to

what Jesus would do, or did do. Will didn't want to give up so easily—
Bud had said he had to do a good job with the small stuff.

"I'm gonna go get a Bible," he said to Fawn. "Don't go away."

"I'm not goin' anywhere," she said. She squeezed her arms
around her legs. "I'm stayin' right here."

Will let himself back in the house and tiptoed into the dining
room where Mom kept the big family Bible on the buffet.

"Don't let me drop this thing," he whispered to God. "Or it'll
wake up half of New Mexico."

Back on the stoop, Will opened the Bible on his lap and flipped
through to Luke. He'd learned from Reverend Bud that most of the
stuff about Jesus' childhood was found in Luke's Gospel. Fawn
waited, sighing impatiently, as Will thumbed through the first few
pages.

"Here it is," he said. He scanned the verses with his eyes. "Okay.
So His mother says to Him, 'Why hast thou thus dealt with us?
Behold thy father and I have sought thee sorrowing.' "

"Huh?" Fawn said.

"It just means why did Jesus do that and get them all worried."

"Oh. Well, why doesn't it just say that?"

"It does." Will shook his head. "Anyway, it goes on—uh—okay,
'And he said unto them—' "

Will looked up at Fawn. "Do you get it so far?"

"Yes! I'm not an idiot!"

"Okay. 'And he said unto them, How is it that ye sought me? Wist
ye not that I must be about my Father's business?' "

"*What?* I don't even know what 'wist' means!"

"I think it means, 'How come you were looking for me? I've got
stuff to do.' "

Fawn's dark eyes narrowed. "So Jesus is saying I oughta tell my
father he should just leave me here to live because I have stuff to do?
I do, you know. I'm supposed to be helping with the horses—"

"Maybe I should read on," Will said. "Uh—'And he went down
with them, and came to Nazareth, and was subject unto them: but
his mother kept all these sayings in her heart.' "

"You're gonna tell me what that means, right?"

"I'm not sure what it means."

"Then how am I supposed to figure it out!?"

"Okay, okay, keep your shirt on." Will studied the verses again. Slowly the words untangled themselves. "Here's what I think it means," he said finally. "He told them He had stuff to do in Jerusalem—you know, so He explained His side—and then He went on ahead and went home and did what they told Him to. Only His mom didn't just drop it. She kept thinking about it."

"So did He ever get to go back to Jerusalem and do what He wanted?" Fawn said.

"Well, yeah, of course He did!"

"Oh, yeah, huh?" Fawn crossed her eyes. "I guess I *am* an idiot."

"Nah," Will said.

He closed the Bible with a soft thud.

"So I still don't get how that tells me what to do," Fawn said.

"Tell your dad how you feel," Will said. "And then go by whatever he says you have to do—only he'll keep thinking about it and probably eventually you'll get to do it—when it's time or something."

Fawn looked at him, her head cocked to one side.

"What?" Will said. "Do I have something in my teeth?"

He was about to poke his finger in his mouth when Fawn shook her head.

"No," she said. "I was just wondering how you got so smart."

"Is this a private party?" someone said. "Or can anybody join?"

Will jumped. So did Fawn. Dan was standing there at the corner of the house. He'd appeared so quietly, Will had no idea how long he'd been there or how much he'd heard.

Fawn untangled herself and got to her feet. Her eyes had a wild look as she watched Dan come toward her.

"I'm sorry," she said in a high-pitched voice Will had never heard her use. "I just wanted to talk to Will for a minute. I wasn't running away or anything—"

"It's all right," Dan said. He stopped on the bottom step and put his hand on her shoulder. "I just missed you, that's all. Wanted to make sure you're all right."

Fawn sank back down to the steps and gave Will a pleading look. Although Dan didn't seem angry to Will at all, Fawn was trembling as though her father had just threatened her with 20 lashes.

"She's all right," Will said. "We were just talking." He gave Fawn a nudge with his knee. "She has something she wants to say to you."

Fawn gave Will her darkest look yet. But Dan sat down beside her and touched her chin, so that she had to look at him.

"If there's something on your mind, chickadee," he said, "I wish you'd tell me."

"I think I oughta let you two talk," Will said.

He started to get up, but Fawn yanked him back down by the leg of his dungarees. "Stay!" she said. "You gotta help me!"

"Help you with what?" her father said.

"With what I want to tell you."

Her father studied her face for a moment, almost as if he were seeing her for the first time.

I guess he is, kind of, Will thought. *She was a whole other person before he left than she is now.* He stifled a grunt. *I've seen her every day, and I still can't figure her out. Maybe it's Dan that needs my help, not her!*

"I guess you're pretty used to having Will around, aren't you?" Dan said. "I can see why. I'd like to have him around myself." He looked at Will. "Do you mind?"

"No," Will said. "Fawn just wants to tell you that she's not so crazy about the idea of moving to Tesuque."

Fawn gave a soft snort.

"Not because she doesn't want to be with you and Conchita," Will went on. "Only because she's used to me, like you said, and Olive and Miguel and Abe."

Fawn jabbed him with her finger.

"But she doesn't want to hurt your feelings," Will said.

She poked him again.

"And she doesn't wanna be disrespectful. She learned that from my mom."

He reached out his hand and caught Fawn's finger before she could jab it into him one last time.

"She'll do whatever you say, but she just wants you to know her side of it."

Fawn nodded, and Will let out a sigh of relief. Dan laughed his deep, booming laugh.

"You two make quite the team!" he said. "I don't know if I can argue much with that."

"Then we can stay here?" Fawn said.

Will poked *her* this time.

"Let me just give you my side of it," Dan said. "Fair enough?"

Fawn shrugged.

"I liked what I saw in Tesuque Village," Dan said. "I like the way it's tucked down among the trees like a secret. Santa Fe has grown since I've been away. I feel a little hemmed in here."

"Oh," Fawn said. "I guess we're going, then."

"For Pete's sake, Fawn!" Will said. "Would you just let him finish?" He looked at Dan. "Women."

Dan's eyes twinkled as he nodded. "I do have a little more to say, if you don't mind," he said to Fawn.

"I guess I don't mind," Fawn said. She jabbed her chin down on her hands again and watched him.

"But one of the things I do like about Santa Fe," Dan went on, "is that the people have banded together during this war to fight the battles you've had to face here."

Will nodded. Bud had just talked about that at the café.

"It's brought the different races together, eased off all that tension I used to sense." Dan nodded at Will and Fawn. "Look at how close the two of you are, Anglo and Indian. Then you have two Hispanics in the mix, Olive and Miguel, and I know you've made friends with some Japanese kids—"

"And don't forget Abe," Fawn said. "He's German."

"Not only that," Dan said, "but the differences among the Indian tribes aren't quite so sharp as they were before. Indians from different pueblos who have come out into the community have had to work together—and I hope that means Quebi will bless your mother's marriage to me now."

Fawn shifted restlessly on the step. "But what's that got to do with us moving to Tesuque?"

"It makes me look at my reasons for wanting to hide away in that little village," Dan said. "A community like Santa Fe never did much for me before the war. I was just a *genizaro*."

"What's that?" Will said.

"An Indian living outside his own group. I didn't belong anywhere. I could forget that when I was drinking, and that's why I never let there be much distance between me and a bottle of whiskey."

Will wasn't sure he got that, but he nodded anyway.

"Even when the war started and I tried to sign up to go, they didn't want Indians." Dan shifted his eyes toward the sky, as if he were seeing a memory up there. "I remember standing in line behind one fella, an Indian. They rejected him because he didn't have any teeth." Dan chuckled. "Fella said, 'I don't want to bite the Germans! I just wanna shoot 'em!' "

Fawn giggled.

"So how did you finally get in?" Will said.

"The army found out they needed us Navajos for a special assignment, and they came looking for us in April '42," he said.

"Wow," Will said. "You musta had an important job."

"I wish I could tell you all about it, but that's classified information. But I *can* tell you that it was just one part of the total effort. And I'll tell you what it did for me: It made me feel like a part of what the whole United States was trying to do. It also showed me that my own culture was absolutely necessary to that effort. I know now that I can live back with my people or outside in the community. I am who I am wherever I am."

"So why can't you be who you are in Santa Fe just as easy as you can in Tesuque?" Fawn said.

Will rolled his eyes again, but Dan smiled softly at Fawn.

"I think I can, chickadee," he said. "You've gotten me to think about it again tonight. I wouldn't have if you hadn't brought it up." He picked up Fawn's hand and flattened it between his. "Besides, you're the whole reason I came home—you and your mother. Every time things got bad over there and I wanted to give up, I'd think about you two back here and I'd keep on fighting to live. It would be kind of silly of me now not to consider your feelings when I'm making decisions."

Fawn turned to look at Will.

"It's works!" she said. "That Jesus thing works!"

Dan gave another one of his booming laughs. "Why don't you tell me about that on the way home, chickadee? Piggyback ride?"

Fawn nodded and climbed onto his back.

"Now, this is not to say we won't ever move to Tesuque," he said as he stood up with her hanging from him. "But you've had a lot of adjustments to make, and I think we need to give you a little time before you have to make more. Meanwhile, you keep hanging out with this guy and your other friends. It's good for you."

"But what about you?" Fawn said.

Will could see Dan holding back a smile. "I'll just have to adjust to the fact that you have other things to do besides hang around with me every minute."

"Yeah," Fawn said solemnly. "I see that."

They both waved to Will and disappeared around the corner of the house. Will leaned against the screen door and closed his eyes. He was happy for Fawn. But it ached in him that Dad wasn't there to hoist Will up onto *his* back.

Fawn had been right, though: the Jesus thing *did* work.

Okay, Jesus, Will thought, his eyes still closed. *Show me what* You *would do if* You *had to wait for* Your *dad while everybody else was getting theirs. I'm paying attention—and I'll do whatever You say.*

He started to go up to his room then, but when he got to the second floor, he looked up and saw a crack of light under the door to the attic. The Marshalls didn't like lights left on at night, Will knew, and he padded up the steps to open the door and snap it off. When he did, he was startled to see a figure with a flashlight bent over a stack of papers on the table.

It was Aunt Hildy Helen.

✠ ⬦ ✠

Chapter Eight

*A*unt Hildy didn't appear to notice him at first. At least she didn't raise her head from whatever it was she was poring over. Will felt a little uneasy. After all, even Bud had said she was really sick—and sick in the head wasn't something he knew a whole lot about.

He was about to close the door and make a hurried exit when she looked up at him. The eyes that seemed too large for her pale, thin face were startled—so startled that they shocked Will.

"Oh!" they both said at once.

"I didn't know you were up here," Will said. "I'll leave you alone—"

"No—it's your house. I'll go—"

She scrambled up and began collecting her papers.

"No, it's okay, really," Will said. "I was just gonna turn out the light."

She stopped tidying and looked at him again in her pale yet startled way. "I can leave," she said.

"No, it's okay," Will said.

She nodded and looked at her papers. Slowly she sat down and shined the flashlight on them again. Will was left standing there, clueless as to whether to leave, which seemed somehow rude, or to try to make conversation, which seemed impossible. He wondered vaguely if Jesus were going to tell him what to do.

"So—" he said finally, "what are you doing?"

She shrugged and picked up a pencil. Will moved closer and craned his neck to see. There was a large, leafless tree drawn on a big piece of paper, and she seemed to be writing names on the various branches. At the top of the paper was the word HUTCHINSON.

"Hey," Will said. "Is that our family tree or somethin'?"

Aunt Hildy nodded without glancing up.

"Where am I?" he said.

"I haven't gotten to you yet," she said.

"Oh." Will edged a little closer to see more. "Josiah Hutchinson. Who's that?"

"One of your ancestors."

Aunt Hildy's voice was flatter than the paper itself. It definitely didn't invite more questions.

I heard you were a hoot when you were younger, Will wanted to say to her. *What happened?*

But he didn't really want to know. What if it was the war that had turned her into a zombie? What if that happened to other people, too—like Dad?

"Guess I'll go to bed," he said to her.

She didn't answer. Will backed toward the door, slipped out of the attic, and closed the door behind him.

"Nice talking to you," he said to himself.

Will didn't see much of his aunt over the next week, although he knew she was still there because he saw the light on in the attic every evening. She seldom came to the table for meals, and the rest of the time Will was at the ranch, grooming the horses and going for rides with Gabby or Señora Otero along.

It wasn't horrible—but it wasn't like the old days when the kids had felt so free on the horses.

"I hate this," Olive muttered to him one day when they were filling up Cisco and Virgy's oat buckets.

"I guess we made a bad choice," Will muttered back.

She looked at him curiously, but Gabby hollered that the horses were hungry, and they didn't finish the conversation.

Sometimes in the evening when Mom and Will were listening to the radio, Aunt Hildy Helen would join them for a few minutes, though she never said anything. She was there the night they got the news that Okinawa had finally been taken by the Allies.

"June 21st," Mom said. "How long has it taken them, Will?" She looked at Aunt Hildy. "Will knows just about everything a civilian can know about the war."

"They started April 1st," Will said. "Almost three months."

Mom shivered. "It must have been horrible."

Aunt Hildy didn't answer. She just got up and left the room.

"What's wrong with her, Mom?" Will said when he heard the attic door close.

"I think the war just got to her," Mom said. "She saw too much horror and she has to find a way to get it out of her mind."

"Is Dad gonna be like that when he comes home?"

Say no, he thought. *Please, Mom, tell me he's not.*

Mom let the bandage she was rolling drop to her lap. "I don't know, son," she said. "All I can say is that I hope not. But if he is, we'll help him get over it."

"By doing what?" Will said. "We haven't been able to do anything for her, so how can we—"

"She's making progress," Mom said. "I've gotten her distracted by suggesting she work on the family tree. It seems to be helping a little. We have to give her time."

It wasn't the answer he wanted to hear.

That night as he lay in bed, praying again for a Jesus-choice, Will decided he knew how Aunt Hildy Helen felt, at least the part about not being able to get something out of her mind. Every time he closed his eyes, he could only see Aunt Hildy's twin brother, his father, sitting in a chair, staring at the tabletop.

I think I need a distraction too, he thought.

Riding the horses certainly wasn't providing one anymore. The kids rode the next morning, Fawn included, but by the afternoon, they were all bored. Without the adventures they used to have, riding had become a chore.

They decided to go back to Santa Fe and see what was going on in town. As usual, the Plaza was sleepy except for the patrons of LaFonda, and even some of them appeared to be dozing over their lemonades and their tortillas. Agent Graves was there, of course, puffing on his pipe. Will observed him with half-interest as the kids settled themselves on the curb across from the hotel.

"Anybody have any money?" Olive said.

There was a unanimous shaking of heads.

"I could sure use some ice cream," she said.

"Chocolate," Fawn said. "Two scoops."

"Quit talking about it," Will said. "You're making it worse."

"What should we talk about, then?" Fawn said.

Will grunted. "Agent Graves."

"Who?" Olive said.

"What is an agent, please?" Miguel said.

"He's the FBI guy," Fawn said, pointing. "He's the one smoking a pipe."

"On such a hot day," Miguel said.

Olive gave Will a nudge. "So what's he doing here, Mr. I Know Everything?"

"I don't know," he said. "I guess he's gathering information."

"Huh," Olive said. "Looks like he's watching the women to me."

"What women?" Will said.

Olive rolled her eyes at Fawn. "Isn't that just like a boy?" she said.

"Yeah," Fawn said.

"What?" Will said.

"It's plain as day that your Agent Graves isn't gathering information—he's looking at that woman with the sun hat, the one with the hibiscus behind her ear."

"What's hibiscus?" Fawn said.

"That red flower," Will said quickly. He didn't want his Mr. I Know Everything status to crumble too much.

"Look at him watching her," Olive said. "I wonder if he wants a date with her."

"Yuck!" Will said.

"He can't even see her face, that hat's so big," Fawn said.

"I do not think he wants a date with the lady," Miguel said.

He pointed to Agent Graves, who had suddenly scraped back his chair and stood up. He dug some change out of his pocket, tossed it on the table, and hurried from the patio, glancing at his watch as he went.

"Wonder where he's going in such a hurry," Fawn said.

Olive gave Will a nudge in the side. "Let's find out," she said.

Will looked at her. "You mean follow him?"

"Sure. What else have we got to do?"

"How will we follow him?" Miguel said. "He has disappeared."

Fawn stood up and looked around, her braids swinging. "Where'd he go?"

"Like I said, let's find out," Olive said. She stood up too, and pulled Will up by his shirt sleeve. "Fawn—you head toward the Cathedral. Miguel, take the Palace. Will—"

"I'll go that way," Will said, pointing toward the Plaza. He wanted to add, *At least let me make up my own mind about something!*

"I'm going to go behind the hotel," Olive said. "Let's meet back here in—"

While she was checking her watch, Will took off down West San Francisco Street and he passed the Trading Post, scanning it through the windows. When he didn't spot Agent Graves shopping for blankets or hominy, he picked up his pace and slipped into the alley that led to West Palace Avenue. Staying low and against the adobe walls made it feel more exciting.

I want to find him without him *seeing* me, he told himself.

But there was no sign of the agent in the alley, nor either way on West Palace. He crossed the street to Grant Avenue, being careful to stay out of view of Reverend Bud's house as he passed it. If Tina Kates saw him, she'd probably call out for him to come in for milk and cookies—and that would blow his cover.

Will smiled to himself. That was a phrase he'd heard in a Humphrey Bogart movie. He'd always wanted to use it.

In order to stay out of the line of sight from the Kateses' windows, he had to cut down another alley, which took him to Sheridan Street, and then made his way back to Grant.

Not that I'm gonna find him there anyway, he thought. But if he didn't see him there, he could always cut back over to Lincoln and meet up with Miguel by the Palace. The two of them always made a good team—

His thoughts stopped dead, however, when he emerged onto Grant Avenue, just in time to see a familiar profile, complete with pipe, crossing the street. Will himself stopped, and stared. Agent Graves appeared to be headed for the back door of First Presbyterian Church.

"What in the world?" Will said out loud.

Agent Graves was going to church? Will's church?

That's funny, Will thought. *I've never seen him at church on a Sunday. Why would he be going on a Friday?*

He could feel a slow smile sliding across his face. It was going to be so good to go back to Olive and announce that he had been the one to track Agent Graves—and to a place nobody would ever have guessed.

And then he grunted. This really was kind of disappointing, when he thought about it. What information-gathering could an FBI agent do in a church?

But Will sighed and crossed the street, still being careful to slide along the church wall once he got there. He had to find out what the man was doing there, or he would never hear the end of it from Olive.

The back door opened into a hallway that ran between the Sunday school building and the church itself. Will stopped just inside and peered through the dimness. There were no windows and he didn't want to risk turning on the light. Still, he could tell that Agent Graves wasn't there.

Whatever he's doing here, Will thought, *he's sure in a hurry to do it.*

Only because it was fun did Will flatten himself against the wall and make his way toward the room at the other end, which he knew was just behind the sanctuary. It was where the choir gathered before the service in their robes so they could file into the church through an arched door.

As soon as he reached the room, Will heard a voice. It was coming from inside the sanctuary. Will knew right away that it was Bud—praying.

Will moved silently to the arched doorway and pressed his ear against the door. Yeah, it was Bud, all right, and there were other people with him, because they all said, "Amen."

Is there some kind of worship service going on? Will thought.

He listened. It was quiet except for the swishing and rustling of what sounded like people changing positions. If only he could see what was going on.

"You've asked me to say a few words today," Will heard Bud say.

"Words to who?" Will muttered to himself.

He looked around the room. There had to be some way to see into the sanctuary from here. Otherwise, how would the choir know when to go into the church?

He slid his hand around the doorway but there were no cracks. Maybe above the door—

Will glanced around for a chair, and his eye fell on a shaft of light that was different from the rest. He grinned at it. A tiny break in the stained glass behind the sanctuary. Perfect for a spying eye.

He had to stand on his toes to reach it, but once he got his balance by leaning against the wall, he could see clearly. When he did, he had to stop himself from crying, "Gotcha!"

There were about a dozen people gathered in the first two pews, all looking expectantly at Reverend Bud who stood just a few feet in front of them. Sitting right in the midst of them, without his pipe, was Agent Graves.

Who knew he believed in Jesus? Will thought. *Huh.*

He studied the other people around him, but none of them looked familiar. They were all Anglos, which was odd. There were so few white people in Santa Fe, Will thought he knew them all.

One thing was for sure, he decided. They all wanted to hear what Reverend Bud had to say. Their eyes were riveted to him as if he were about to expose some secret they'd all been dying to know about. It made Will listen more closely.

It was actually hard to make out most of it. Bud was keeping his voice low, and it sounded earnest and serious. Only a few words were clear to Will—

"I understand—"

"—a difficult choice to make—"

What he was saying didn't seem to be that earth-shaking, as far as Will was concerned. Not until the phrase that burned into his brain like a brand.

"From what I know," Bud said, "about the Manhattan Project—"

✢ ✤ ✢

Chapter Nine

*W*ill couldn't get out of the church fast enough. He didn't even care if anyone heard him as he ran down the hall and out into the churchyard. There was no more flattening himself against walls like a spy as he plowed down Palace Avenue.

So Bud does know about the Manhattan Project after all, Will thought. *I wonder if he thought about what Jesus would do before he lied to me.*

That made Will feel even worse. Bud had also said he didn't know anything about the FBI man. *But how can he not—he's part of his little private prayer meeting! Wait'll I tell Fawn and Olive and Miguel—*

But that thought slowed him down at the corner of Lincoln and Palace. It was a choice. He leaned against the adobe wall and tried to get all of his thoughts into one pile from where they were scattered all over his mind.

If I tell them, then they're all gonna know he's a liar. Would Jesus do that?

On the other hand, why shouldn't they know that? They all trust him too, just like I do. Jesus exposed bad people all the time in the Bible.

But that wouldn't stay put in Will's head. Bud—a bad person? Just because he didn't tell everything he knew?

All that means is that he doesn't trust me, Will thought.

It was a thought that bent his shoulders into a sag. And it wasn't one he wanted to share with anybody else.

I hope this is the choice You would make, Jesus, he thought. *I'm not telling anybody about this.*

But that didn't mean he didn't talk to himself about it, almost nonstop, even when he rounded everybody up and told them half the truth—that he'd seen Agent Graves going into the church.

Olive, of course, wanted to know why. Will just shrugged. It was partially true—he really didn't know what the prayer meeting was about. Why encourage even more questions?

Although he hadn't been looking forward to Dan and Conchita's wedding all that much, considering the fancy suit they were making him wear, Will was almost glad it was the next day. It kept everybody from bugging him about Agent Graves, and kept him from thinking about Bud quite so much.

It was hard, though, when he got to the church and Bud clapped him on the back and told him he looked "sharp" in his tuxedo. He questioned in his mind whether Bud was telling him the truth even about that.

"You okay, my friend?" Bud said.

He searched Will's face with his eyes. Will avoided them. "Sure," he said. "Why wouldn't I be?"

But just before Fawn left the back room to go around to the front of the church, where she would enter just ahead of her mother, Will took her aside.

"Are you sure I don't look stupid?" he said.

Fawn looked at him almost shyly. "I think you look kind of handsome," she said.

"You didn't have to go that far," Will said.

"Yeah, well, don't let it give you a big head," she said back.

He felt a little better.

But once he and Dan stepped out to the front of the altar with

Bud beside them and Fawn and Conchita coming up the aisle—
Conchita in the dress made from Dan's parachute that everyone kept
saying was "exquisite"—Will couldn't stop thinking about Bud.

What if he isn't really a minister? he thought when Bud had said
his first, "Let us pray," and all heads bowed. *What if he really belongs
to the FBI and that whole prayer meeting was a cover for some case
they're working on?*

Or what if Agent Graves wasn't really an agent—and all those
people at the meeting in the church were spies themselves, including
Bud?

Will sneaked a glance at Bud, who was praying with one hand on
Dan's shoulder and the other on Conchita's, and he almost laughed
out loud. Bud with his chubby pink cheeks and pudgy mouth, a spy?
He couldn't pull off a surprise party with that face; it gave everything
away. Right now, for instance, there was nothing but love and hope
glowing from every pore—

The laughter died in Will's throat. Bud was the best person he
knew in the world. He'd adopted a retarded boy, for Pete's sake, and
how many times had he rescued the kids from their own stupid mistakes and cried with Mom when she was torn up about Dad—

No, Will thought as heads lifted and Bud beamed at the ring Will
handed him for Conchita. Whatever the Manhattan Project was, it
must be pretty important for Bud to lie about it. He could only be
keeping it a secret to protect somebody.

I gotta forget about it, Will thought. *I gotta think about something else.*

He focused on the ceremony. "You may kiss the bride," Bud said.

As Dan leaned over to kiss Conchita, Will squeezed his eyes shut.
Okay, maybe something *else.*

When Conchita and Dan marched down the aisle to the strains of
joyous music from the organ, it was finally over. Will started to follow
Bud toward the back room, thinking that now would be a good time
to apologize to him for being cold to him before the service.

"*Psst*—Will!"

Will looked up to see Fawn waving him toward her.

"What?" he hissed back at her.

"You're supposed to walk down the aisle with me, remember?"

Will stifled a groan. This was the part he hadn't been too happy about at the rehearsal last night. Fawn hadn't seemed too keen on it then either, but now that she was dressed in pink and had a bow in her hair, she seemed willing to slip her hand over his arm and coax him down the aisle.

It was the single most embarrassing thing that had ever happened to him, made more so by the smirk on Olive's face when they passed her. The only thing that kept Will from stopping to threaten her was the fact that her father was sitting next to her.

They gave him a pass from the sanitarium to come to the wedding? Will thought. That was odd. Eduardo Fernandez didn't even know the McHorses.

Of course, there *was* the reception at the Pink Adobe afterward. Will had already told Olive he wasn't dancing. He decided that maybe she'd brought her father along so she'd have a partner.

As soon as they were out the front door, Will snatched himself away from Fawn and headed for the back room.

"Where are you going?" Fawn said.

"I gotta talk to Reverend Bud."

"We're having our pictures taken," she said.

Will stared at her in horror. They were going to take a *picture* of the two of them arm in arm?

"Can't you do it without me?" Will said, backing away.

"I need you, Will!" Dan called over to him. "You aren't going to leave me with all these women, are you, buddy?"

Fawn smiled sweetly and held out her hand to Will. He let her loop it around his arm and tried not to grit his teeth. She couldn't get out of that pink dress and back into her dungarees soon enough, as far as he was concerned. He'd rather have her pounding on him.

The picture-taking session took so long, Will checked to see if he were growing a beard yet. Everybody else had gone on to the Pink Adobe, including Mom and Aunt Hildy Helen and Margretta and Olive and Mr. T. and the Señora and Miguel.

"You can ride with us, Will," Fawn said. "Mr. T. arranged for horses and an old-fashioned carriage!"

"But that leaves me all alone!" Reverend Bud said.

Will jumped. He hadn't even been aware that Bud had come back into the church. He was out of his robe and fiddling with his necktie. He looked as uncomfortable as Will felt.

"Why doesn't Will ride with me?" he said. "I just have a few things to take care of in the back room and we'll be right along."

Fawn looked as if she might protest, but her father held out his arm for her to put her hand on and she let him glide her happily down the aisle.

"What is with her and the arm stuff?" Will said to Bud when they were out of earshot.

"Girls love that kind of thing," Bud said. "I've never figured it out."

"Thanks for saving me," Will said. "And Reverend Bud, I just wanted to say—"

"Forget it," Bud said. "We're all a little on edge these days. Why don't you wait for me out here? I won't be a minute." He lowered his voice to a whisper. "If you'll lose your tie, I'll lose mine."

They grinned at each other, and Bud disappeared into the room behind the sanctuary. Will sank to the steps in front of the altar and worked at the bow tie with his fingers.

I'm glad my parents already had a church wedding, he thought. *Because I'm never wearing one of these again for anybody.*

The thing was hard to get off, and Will was about to head for the back room to get Bud to undo it for him, when he heard a loud voice coming from that very direction. At first Will thought it was Bud, fooling around as he tried to get his own necktie off. But the voice wasn't Bud's. It took Will a moment to realize it belonged to Olive's father, Eduardo Fernandez.

"Don't think nobody knows about your little secret services, Reverend," Eduardo was practically shouting. It didn't sound like yelling, actually. It was more like a voice that had simply gone out of control. As far as Will could tell, all those weeks in the sanitarium weren't doing much good.

"Mr. Fernandez," Bud said in a tone that reminded Will of someone soothing a cranky baby. "It is my job as associate pastor of this church to provide services for anyone who needs them. I am available to all people."

"Does that include suspicious people? People with war business?" Will sat up straighter on the bench and abandoned the necktie.

"We are a nation at war, Mr. Fernandez," Bud said. "I know you are against the war, but it is still being fought. I can't ignore the people who are involved in the effort—"

"Even if those people are building weapons of mass destruction?" Eduardo's voice went shrill, like a fingernail being dragged down a chalkboard. It dragged down Will's spine and left him with chills.

Weapons of mass destruction? What was he talking about?

"It's bad enough we have soldiers over there," Eduardo went on, his voice still piercing. "I can't do anything to change that. But to have war business going on right here under our noses, and for you to sanction it with prayer—"

"The Church is an instrument of Christ's compassion and love," Bud said, "and its benefits are for everyone."

"Everyone. So that includes scientists who are creating something that will destroy thousands of lives? It was one thing to develop such a weapon when we feared the Germans had come up with something similar that would win the war for them, but they have already been defeated. There is no need for it now, and yet those project people go on building a weapon that could annihilate an entire race!"

"That is only a rumor."

Bud's voice was no longer kind. It was firm, as though that cranky baby he'd been soothing now needed to be scolded and sent off to its room.

"I heard it from a reliable source," Eduardo said.

"Forgive me, sir," Reverend Bud said, "but would that be a source inside the sanitarium where you are now living because you have been deemed to be out of touch with reality?"

Eduardo Fernandez then exploded into a frenzy of Spanish, which Will was glad he couldn't understand. He was relieved when he heard Bud ushering him out the door and into the hall, but his own thoughts stirred up anxiety like silt from the bottom of a pond.

Eduardo's talking about the Manhattan Project. I already know Bud's mixed up in it somehow—

Bud—his trusted friend—the man who would turn himself inside out to get Will out of trouble.

And it sounded like Bud might be in the deepest kind of trouble.

It sounded like he didn't believe Eduardo, he thought. *It sounded like he didn't know any of that stuff about mass destruction and thousands of people being killed.*

Maybe Bud hadn't been lying to Will at all. Maybe he was just being the good, trusting Bud everybody knew—just letting people come together for prayer about something he didn't even ask questions about.

But what if Eduardo is right and it's going to hurt innocent people? Will thought. *Shouldn't Bud know? Shouldn't he have all the information?*

Something else struck Will then, like a jagged bolt of lightning. Bud had gotten very upset when Will had talked about Los Alamos and told him he and the other kids had been up there. Was the Manhattan Project going on up at Los Alamos?

But if it is, he doesn't know what it's all about. Maybe he asked, only they wouldn't tell him. Maybe they told him the same thing he told us: to just stay away from it.

The thoughts shouted at Will, tearing from one side of his mind to the other until suddenly they came together in a single choice, clear and sharp and all too obvious: *Do I leave this alone and let Bud figure it out, or do I try to find out what I can so he doesn't get hurt?*

Yes, Bud had told them to stay away from Los Alamos. And yes, the soldier had warned them never to come back there. But did he— and the other kids—have to *go* there to find out what was happening? Bud himself had let it slip that the Project had an office right here in Santa Fe. If they could find out where that office was now, if they could pretend to be just being kids while they kept their ears and their eyes open, would that be disobeying anybody's orders?

Will looked up at the cross which hung stark and clear above the sanctuary. "Jesus?" he whispered. "What would You do?"

"What would He do about what, my friend?" someone said.

It was Bud, smiling down at him, ready to help him with anything—anything at all.

"Thanks anyway," Will said. "But I think I've figured it out."

✛ ⚜ ✛

Chapter Ten

*E*duardo Fernandez didn't show up at the Pink Adobe for the reception, and that was fine with Will. But it did leave him wondering what to do about Olive. Should he tell her what he'd heard her father say to Bud? And if he didn't, how was he going to act around her? That was one choice that seemed very clear: He would just avoid her until he figured it out.

He managed to do that by ducking around piles of wedding gifts and spending a lot of time in the men's room. But he had a lapse as he stopped, mouth watering, to watch Conchita and Dan cut into their wedding cake, and Olive herself came up beside him and nudged him with her elbow.

"Where's Fawn?" she said.

Will stiffened. "How should I know?" he said. "I hope she's changing her clothes. Ever since she put that stupid dress on she's been acting weird."

"So I noticed."

Olive slid her hand through Will's arm. When he jerked it away, she threw her head back and laughed.

"I don't see what's so funny," Will said. "It was a pain in the neck having her hanging all over me."

"I don't know—I thought it was kind of sweet."

Will started to glare at her, but her eyes were sparkling.

"She comes by it honestly," she said. "Look at her parents, making googly eyes at each other."

Will watched as Conchita put her hand over Dan's as he cut the first piece of wedding cake.

"She doesn't think he can cut a piece of cake by himself?" Will said.

"It's tradition," Olive said.

"Looks pretty mushy to me." Will shot her a look. "And don't get any ideas about helping me cut my piece."

"Well, at least you wouldn't be hiding from me then."

Will could feel his face going red. He was about as good at this clandestine stuff as Bud was.

"So what's going on?" she said. "Do I have bad breath? Body odor?"

"No," Will said. "I don't even know what you're talking about. I'm just busy doing stuff."

Olive shook her head. "You couldn't lie your way out of a paper bag, Will Hutchinson. Tell me why you're avoiding me like I have leprosy, or I'll make it very *easy* for you to avoid me."

"I'm not—"

"Then forget it," she said. And she marched away with a toss of her black mane, which, he saw, was tied in several places with pink bows.

Pink, he decided, was the curse of the day.

He was mulling that over when Dan appeared at his side, still wiping frosting from his upper lip.

"Don't you want some cake?" he said.

Will shook his head. He'd completely lost his appetite.

"So," Dan said, "what are you doing Monday?"

"Probably nothing," Will said. "Half my friends are now mad at me."

"Let's see what we can do about that. Why don't you and Miguel come with us up to San Ildefonso? Conchita and I are going to try to make peace with Quebi."

"For real?" Will said. "We can go up to the Pueblo?"

"I understand you and Quebi are friends. This will give you a chance to see him." Dan shrugged. "Who knows, maybe you can put in a good word for me, huh?"

Will grinned, though not about Quebi. He would love to talk to Fawn's grandfather; he always did. But the San Ildefonso Pueblo wasn't far from Los Alamos. He and Miguel and maybe Fawn could climb the mesa and possibly get another look from there. No soldiers were going to be patrolling the Pueblo.

"So, you like the idea?"

Dan was studying his face and grinning. Will nodded. "Yeah," he said. "I like it a lot."

Dan nodded and then surveyed the crowd. "Olive!" he said. "Come here, would you? I want to ask you something."

Will immediately shook his head, but Olive had already answered Dan's call and was nodding as Dan talked to her.

"I'd love to come," Will heard her say. Then she directed her eyes at Will. "If nobody minds, that is."

I do *mind!* Will wanted to say to her. *I'm just trying to keep you from getting your feelings hurt, that's all.*

"Well?" she said.

"Are you talking to me?" Will said.

"Yes. Do you mind if I go to the Pueblo with all of you?"

"Mind? Why should I mind?"

Olive cocked an eyebrow. "Don't quit your day job to become a spy, Will. You'll never make it." Then she smiled at Dan and said, "Count me in."

That's okay, Will thought as she tossed her hair—and her pink bows—and went off to join Fawn. *I'll just find a way to get off alone with Miguel.*

The group set out early Monday morning for San Ildefonso, both to beat the early-July heat and to stay ahead of the electrical storm that was predicted to roll down from the Jemez Mountains that afternoon.

They had to take two cars, and Will tried to squeeze into Bud's jalopy of a Chevy with him and Tina and Abe and Mom. But Fawn insisted he ride in Margretta Dietrich's car with her and Dan and Conchita and Miguel—and Olive.

You'd think me and Olive were Siamese twins, he thought miserably. His plan to get Miguel off by himself and hike up the mesa without her was getting more unrealistic by the minute.

It was a dry morning so far, and Will pretended to be studying the irrigation ditches out the car window so he would have an excuse not to talk to Olive.

"New Mexico never has enough water," he announced to the group, just to make his guise more believable. "See, the Mariposa lilies are blooming. They haven't bloomed in three years—it's taken them that long to get enough moisture."

Olive sniffed. He had a feeling he wasn't fooling her at all.

But she obviously wasn't going to let it ruin her day. She propped her elbows on the back of the front seat and fired questions at Margretta and Dan.

"So, tell me again why we're making this trip. I didn't quite understand it when Dan said he was going to try to get somebody's blessing." She gave her hair the usual toss. "When I'm an adult, I am going to make my *own* decisions."

Margretta smiled in the rearview mirror. "I have no doubt about that, Olive. But with the Pueblo Indians, it's a little different."

Dan twisted around so he could look at Olive from the front seat. "See, San Ildefonso is a Tanoan Pueblo, and it's where Conchita grew up. I'm Navajo. By and large, the Pueblo Indians haven't integrated and intermarried with Anglos *or* with people of other tribes."

"You are all fortunate to be given this opportunity, by the way," Margretta said. "The Pueblos preserve a secretive and closely guarded barrier against all outsiders."

"I prefer to call it a cocoon," Dan said. "It's how they've preserved their traditions and customs."

"So—you've turned Conchita into a butterfly!" Olive said.

Dan gave Conchita what Olive would call a "googly" smile. "I like to think so," he said.

Will rolled his eyes as he continued to fake observing the *acequias* leading water off to the alfalfa fields.

"But it *has* created its problems," Dan went on. "Not only did Conchita marry someone not from her Pueblo—but she married a man who did not live with his own tribe. Ever since I was 16, I've tried to live away from the reservation. I even came here from western New Mexico to get away from it."

"So it's worse than, say, me marrying Will," Olive said. "An Anglo and a Hispanic."

"What?" Will said. He whipped around from the window to see Olive giving him a triumphant look. She'd caught him listening.

"Yuck!" Fawn said.

At least Fawn's back to normal, Will thought. He turned back and nearly pressed his nose against the glass.

"And then to make matters worse," Margretta was saying, "when Conchita was diagnosed with her eye disease, her father—that's Quebi—could not understand why she wanted to go to an Anglo hospital instead of relying on the Pueblo's healers and remedies."

"One of the things I learned in the war, one of the many things," Dan said, "is that all of us—Plains and Pueblo Indians—should turn more to modern medicine. I'm not saying we should abandon our traditional beliefs. The healers have good, sound advice based on their knowledge of their people. But I believe we should use patent medicines and have vaccinations."

"Shots," Fawn said. "I hate shots."

Olive gave a hurried nod. "So—you're hoping you can get all this straightened out with—what's his name?"

"Quebi," Dan said. "I want to convince him that God smiles on my marriage to Conchita and on Fawn, and that there is no need for there to be this bad blood between us. I would love to spend time on the Pueblo. I love it there."

"Just let me warn you," Margretta said. "A lot has changed since the war started. The Pueblo has really felt the absence of the men who have either gone off to the army or gotten jobs in the cities. The women had to do all the planting and harvesting and herd the livestock."

"I bet they did a marvelous job, too," Olive said. "Right, Fawn?"

Fawn gave a firm nod. Will did turn from the window then to exchange disgusted glances with Miguel. He wondered vaguely what Jesus would do with these women.

"They ran out of tires," Margretta went on. "The school bus service was cancelled, so most of the children have stopped going to school. Everyone has had to walk miles for supplies. Some of the agency buildings have had to close—"

"But the beauty is still the same," Dan said. He leaned forward to peer out the windshield. "I can see it already as we get closer."

Will could see it too. He stopped pretending to be concerned about irrigation and took in the scenery he hadn't seen in a while—scenery that always made him peaceful.

San Ildefonso was in the Rio Grande Valley, at the broad mouth of the Rio Nambé, whose water now barely reached the Rio Grande. The rounded hills that guarded the Pueblo to the east were dotted with ovals of piñon and juniper, while to the west the Black Mesa stood square and solid at the margin of the river, a plum-colored table of hardened lava. The people on the Pueblo lived in a landscape that stretched in all directions, even toward the sky.

But I have to keep my focus today, he told himself. *I have to find out more about Los Alamos, and this is my only chance.*

Olive continued to ask questions as Margretta steered the car into the pueblo-maze of dirt roads and alleys, outside ovens, and corrals.

"So—the people live in those houses?" she said, pointing to the row of adobe buildings that bordered one of the two "plazas."

They weren't like the grassy, shaded Plaza in Santa Fe, however. They were just two wide-open fields of dirt with one large cottonwood tree, but no non-Indians were allowed on them.

There were several women outside as the two cars sent dust flying with their entrance. When they saw Margretta, their solemn faces broke into smiles and they hurried toward her, chattering in the Tewa language in their soft, low voices. Will grinned to himself, thinking how loud Olive was going to seem among them.

Some other women waved from against an adobe building where they were coiling and pinching clay for pottery.

"I've always wanted to see how they did that," Olive said as she climbed from the car and shaded her eyes with her hand to gaze at them.

An idea sparked in Will's head. "You should go watch them," he said. "They might be making polychrome—that's the black-on-black stuff that's really famous. They excavate their own clay and everything." It was all he could do not to give her a shove. "Go watch," he said again.

To his relief, she seemed about to dash toward them, with a million questions ready, he was sure.

But Margretta called to them from the direction of Quebi's earthen house.

"Come eat first," she said. "It's not polite to skip the meal."

Will wanted to answer that Olive wasn't hungry, but she was already headed toward the smell of fry bread. There was nothing to do but follow.

The group was already gathering outside Quebi's house, though the old grandfather himself had not joined them. Will noticed that Conchita was back to her old, timid self, only now Dan was next to her, whispering in her ear and making her smile and sit up straighter on the ground.

Everyone else was watching the Indian women pull pots from the fire with long, thin poles and exclaiming over the smells. Will tried not to squirm too much. He knew that serving food on the Pueblo was always orderly and polite—and slow—and he and Miguel had things to do.

A woman with a very square haircut, who Will thought might be Conchita's sister, was serving each person, one by one—first the guests, then her husband, then all the children in order of age, and finally herself.

Will gobbled down the beans and chilis as fast as his throat would let him, but he still had to wait for his turn to return the empty dish to the server with the appropriate word of thanks.

This, he thought, *takes longer than Thanksgiving.*

Although he was thinking about how soon he and Miguel could slip away, he did notice how different Fawn was on this visit than he had seen her before at the Pueblo. She talked in a soft, low voice and didn't jump around or threaten to pound Will even once. She just kept looking at Dan with affection, and the other Indians were smiling as they watched her.

I hope that helps with Quebi, Will thought. He remembered, guiltily, that he was supposed to "put in a good word" for Dan. He'd been concentrating too hard on making a Los Alamos sighting to even think about it. A glance at Bud, however, reminded him of what was really important today.

It was customary to stay seated until everyone had finished the meal. With Abe there, that took a while. The Indian women were delighted each time he presented his bowl and said, "More, please?"

"We should teach him how to say it in Tewa," Fawn said.

"Oh, let's don't confuse him," Tina said, patting her big son's arm. "He has enough trouble with English."

Then she kissed Abe soundly on the cheek. Will looked quickly at the Indians. It wasn't their custom to show affection in public. But the women seemed too intrigued by Abe's appetite to care.

I care! Will thought. *Hurry up, Abe—or it's gonna be time to go home!*

Finally, Abe polished off yet another bowl of beans and presented it to the women to be filled—and they had to show him the empty pot to convince him that there was no more left.

"Come on, honey," Tina said. "We'll find something else fun to do."

You do that, Will thought. *And Miguel and I will go up to the mesa and the girls will—*

He looked nervously at Olive. She had stood up and was gazing out over the plazas.

"There's a lot to see," he said. "I've pretty much seen it all—but Fawn could show you around."

"You could take Abe, too, then," Tina said. "I'm sure he'd love a tour."

Will held his breath. Fawn could be pretty stubborn sometimes. But she nodded and said, "Let's go. I'll show you all my favorite spots."

The two girls started off. But Abe hung back, looking longingly at Will.

"What's wrong, pal?" Will said. "Catch up with the girls or you're going to miss everything."

Abe hung his head sadly.

"What?" Will said. He was trying not to sound impatient, but it was hard.

"Abey go with Will," Abe said finally.

"You can't," Will said.

"Why can't he?" Olive said. She and Fawn had stopped and were standing with their hands on their hips. Will wanted to groan out loud.

"I thought he wanted to learn about stuff," Will said. "He needs to be up there with Fawn so he can hear what she's saying."

Even Miguel looked puzzled at that explanation. Abe "learning stuff" was usually the last thing on anybody's mind.

"I just want him to get the most out of his day up here," Will said. He gave Abe a gentle shove. "Go on, pal. I'll see you soon."

Abe gave him a last, wistful look and then stumbled off toward Olive and Fawn like a reluctant bear. Will felt a guilty pang, but he pushed it firmly away. He was doing this for Bud—and that meant it was for Abe's good, too.

Fawn, Olive, and Abe started off again. Will caught Miguel by the sleeve to keep him from following and was just about to fill him in when Fawn turned and said, "You guys *are* coming, right?"

Abe looked pathetically hopeful. Olive didn't say a word or even cock an eyebrow. She only looked back at him, and for an instant, he caught a glimmer of something in her eyes. He didn't know if it was hope or hurt.

"Sure," he said. "We're comin'."

Olive then gave her hair its usual toss and set out next to Fawn, bombarding her with questions. Abe lumbered along behind them, smiling just because he was with his friends. Will caught Miguel's sleeve again and slowed his steps.

"First chance we get," he whispered, "we slip away and head for the mesa."

"Why?" Miguel whispered back.

"I'll tell you when we get away from them."

At first that didn't seem very likely. Olive's questions had Fawn turning and pointing in every direction, which made it impossible for Will and Miguel to sneak away unnoticed. It wasn't until Olive asked to see the inside of a *horno*—one of the igloo-like ovens the women cooked in—that Will saw their chance. While Fawn, Olive, and Abe got on all fours to peer inside it, Will jerked his head at Miguel and they ducked behind the nearest adobe. The Black Mesa beckoned just behind them.

"When I say go, just make a run for those trees," Will whispered.

Miguel nodded.

Why can't girls be more like boys? Will thought. *We don't stand around asking a bunch of questions.*

Making a mental note to thank Miguel for that later, Will hissed, "Go!" They took off across a clearing, dodging a couple of scrawny chickens who didn't even lift their heads from the dirt they were pecking at. When they got to the cottonwoods, Will flung himself behind one thick trunk and peered around it. Fawn, Abe, and Olive were nowhere in sight. Trying not to think about the half-hurt, half-hopeful look in Olive's eyes, or the sadness in Abe's, Will put his lips close to Miguel's ear.

"On the count of three we make a run for the mesa," he whispered. "Then we just try to stay in the crevices so they don't see us."

"All right, my friend," Miguel said. "But be careful. That is lava. It will make you slip."

Will nodded as he looked at the flat-topped, rocky-sided height they were about to climb. It didn't matter how many times he slipped. He had to make it to the top and get a look at Los Alamos.

All remained still from behind them. Unless Fawn and Olive had gotten rid of Abe somehow, there was no way that they could sneak up on the boys and catch them by surprise. Will counted under his breath: "One—two—go!"

The two of them took off across the clearing. There was nothing to hide behind but plenty to trip on. Will tried to watch his footing as he dodged clumps of *chamisa* and *gramma* grass, but he still caught the leg of his dungarees on a cactus and had to stifle a yelp.

Ahead of him Miguel stopped on a plateau-like piece of rock that jutted out from the side of the mesa and pointed to the mountain's flat top.

"What?" Will said.

"It would take a very long time for us to reach the top, my friend," Miguel said. "Perhaps you can see what you want to see from here."

Will dragged his arm across his mouth and licked his lips. The air was so dry, he already felt as if he'd been chewing on a wad of cotton. He knew Miguel was probably right, and he nodded.

"We can see some of Los Alamos from here, anyway."

Miguel's dark brows came together in a frown. "I thought we were done with that."

"We were—but I sure wish we could get up there for a better look. I don't think Bud really knows what he's getting into." He gave Miguel a quick look. "Ya gotta trust me, all right? I don't want to get you in trouble by, y'know, telling you too much. It's not like I know very much myself, but I've—well, I've made a choice to try to help Bud."

"We will look, then," Miguel said. Again, he pointed upward. "Perhaps we can climb a little higher."

He didn't ask another question as they climbed like spiders from one narrow, rocky plateau to another, stopping only long enough to try to work up some saliva and spit out the dust.

At one point, Will stopped and turned to Miguel, his fingers curled around a jutting piece of rock.

"Miguel?" he said. "Do you think this is the way the soldiers felt when they were climbing Mt. Suribachi? You know, at Iwo Jima?"

"Perhaps," Miguel said.

"Okay, then," Will said. "If they could do it, we can. We're doin' it for our country, just like they did."

He started to resume the climb, but Miguel put his hand on Will's arm.

"What?" Will said.

"*Shh!*"

Miguel put his finger to his lips and cocked his head. Will listened too, and he heard something faint, maybe a voice, maybe a piece of rock knocked loose from its place and tumbling down the mountainside.

"Is someone coming?" Will whispered.

Miguel closed his eyes, trying to shut out everything but the sound, which Will could no longer hear. He shook his head.

"I think it is nothing," Miguel said.

"Then let's keep climbing," Will said.

And so they went on. But they had only made it halfway up the Black Mesa when Will began to feel light-headed. He perched himself on a shelf of a rock, and Miguel joined him.

"We need a rest, my friend," Miguel said.

"Just a short one. Hey, Miguel—" Will pointed to the Pajarito Plateau. "There it is! There's Los Alamos! We can just see it from here."

Miguel shaded his eyes and followed Will's point. "I see," he said. "And now will you tell me why it is so important that we know about this Los Alamos?"

"Yeah, Will," said another voice. "Why don't you tell all of us?"

Will jerked around, nearly toppling from his rock-seat. It was Olive, flattened against the lava wall. Just below her were Abe and Fawn.

Chapter Eleven

*W*ill knew he was staring at Olive and the others, open-mouthed and bug-eyed. The choice was right in front of him: forget the whole thing and protect Olive, or tell them everything and help Bud. But he didn't know which way to go.

"All right, Jesus," he muttered under his breath. "Tell me what You'd do."

"I think He'd tell you to start spilling your guts to your friends," Olive said.

"You have ears like an alley cat," Will said. "I wasn't even talking to you."

"Well, you'd better start."

Olive folded her arms. Just below her, Fawn made her way around so she could face the boys with eyes narrowed down to little points. Abe, on the other hand, stayed where he was and looked down at the ground, *his* eyes the size of dinner plates.

"It's okay, pal," Will said to him. "Just stay where you are and you won't fall." He glared at Fawn. "Why did you let him come up here? Look at him; he's scared to death!"

"As if we could have stopped him," Olive said. "He wanted to be where you were. In case you haven't noticed, he worships the ground you walk on—so don't change the subject, which is: What are you doing up here? Why are you still trying to spy on Los Alamos?"

Will bit at his lip. Jesus wasn't talking yet. Nobody was carrying a Bible. And as for somebody wise to advise him—he was on his own.

Jesus would— what? Make up a lie?

Will shook his head at Olive. "I can't tell you," he said.

"But you can tell Miguel."

"He has not told me, *mi amiga*," Miguel said.

"Well, unlike you, I'm not willing to just follow Will around without knowing what's going on," Olive said. "And neither is Fawn."

Fawn shook her head. She hadn't taken her eyes off of Will once.

Only Abe seemed happy with Will at the moment, but his smile was trembly as he said, "Hi!"

"Hi, pal," Will said. He sighed. "Okay, look. I heard some more stuff about Los Alamos—something that might get . . . somebody . . . in trouble."

"What somebody?" Olive said. "Who?"

Will darted his eyes to Abe.

"It's going to get Abe in trouble?" she said.

Abe gave a startled jerk, which nearly sent him tumbling down the side of the mesa. "Abey?" he said. "Abey bad?"

"No, for Pete's sake!" Will said. He turned to Olive, his teeth clenched together. "Would you hush up about it? I promise I'll tell you later. It has something to do with B-U-D."

"Bud's in trouble?" Fawn said. "He can't be in trouble—he's the preacher!"

Abe stood straight up, his toes hanging over the narrow ledge. "Bud?" he said. "My dad? My dad bad?"

Will put his hands over his ears and squeezed his eyes shut. "Girls! They're driving me nuts, Miguel! Save me, would ya?"

"Abey save Will!" Abe cried. "My dad bad? Will—trouble?" He tossed his big head, his eyes wild with confusion. "Abey save!"

"No, pal. I'm okay!" Will said.

But Abe was already hurling himself across the rocks toward Will, his arms stretched out to "save" him.

"Stop, Abe, you big oaf!" Fawn cried. She made a lunge for Abe, but she was only able to clutch at his pant leg. It was enough to make him stagger. One big foot slipped on the hardened lava and brought him down on his tailbone.

Careening like a toboggan, Abe slid downhill on his seat. Olive made a grab for him but she missed. Will was above him and could only stand helplessly by as Abe headed straight for the side and its 50-foot drop.

"Stop him, Miguel!" Olive screamed.

Tiny Miguel had already thrown himself onto Abe's back, and Will felt a shot of hope as his slight weight slowed Abe down. Instead of shooting straight over the edge, the two of them rolled to the side and bumped over a downward slope of jagged rocks. Together they crashed into a spiked formation of stone and lay dead still.

Olive, Fawn, and Will crawled like frightened crabs to get to them. Olive reached them first and put her hand on Miguel's back, babbling to him in frantic Spanish.

"I am fine," Miguel told her. "I am fine."

"How could you possibly be fine? Let me see your face!"

Miguel pulled himself gingerly away from Abe and looked up at Olive. His face was cloud white, but he did look fine to Will. But not so Abe.

"He's awful quiet," Fawn said.

Will picked his way past Olive and Miguel and knelt next to his pal. There was no yelping, no whimpering, no crying out that "Abey" was "bad." Abe lay limp against the row of spiked rocks he had crashed into, eyes closed, lips blue.

"Will, he's not dead, is he?" Fawn said. "Is he dead?"

"Fawn—quiet!" Olive said.

Will put his face next to Abe's. Shallow breath tickled his nose.

"He's breathing!" Will said. "He's okay!"

"He is bleeding, my friend."

Will looked where Miguel was pointing. A trail of blood was running from the back of Abe's head down onto his neck. Another trickle dripped from his ear.

"We have to get him back," Olive said. "He needs a doctor or a healer—or something—"

"He should not be moved," Miguel said. "I know that with people hurt—he should not be moved."

"He's right, Will," Olive said. "One of us needs to go get help."

"I'll go," Fawn said. "I'm the fastest."

"No," Will said. "It's my fault—"

"Both of you go," Olive said, barking the words out. "Fawn can run ahead and get them started up here with help, and Will, you can stay there and explain everything."

For once Will was glad to have someone else do the choosing. As Fawn picked her way to a spot where she could start her climb down the mesa, Will crouched beside Abe again.

"Hang on, pal," he whispered to him. "We'll get help. You'll be okay. And I'm—I'm really sorry."

"Go, Will," Olive said. Her voice was softer now, and so were her eyes. "Just go."

The climb down the mesa was a series of bumps and scrapes and slides that Will was sure were going to send *him* crashing against the rocks. But the thought of Abe lying up there motionless and pale blue kept him praying and kept him moving.

Fawn reached the bottom long before he did. In the distance he could see her darting among the Pueblo buildings like a rabbit. By the time he joined her, it was obvious she had told the adults everything. Margretta was already on the way to the tribal president's office to use the only phone on the Pueblo to call for an ambulance. Conchita was speaking in rapid Tewa to an older Indian Will knew was a healer. Dan and Bud ripped past Will, their arms full of ropes and blankets, their eyes full of concern.

Will looked around for his mother, and his heart sank. She was sitting on the ground with her arms around Tina, who was crying like Will had never seen a grown-up cry before. He couldn't even imagine Jesus getting Himself into this situation.

His feet feeling like lead, Will walked over to them and squatted down. Tina's face was buried in Mom's shoulder.

"I bet he's gonna be okay," Will said. "He was breathing when I left him. And there wasn't that much blood. I'm thinking he's gonna be fine."

Tina lifted her head and gave Will a tear-filled glare. "Why did you take him up there? You know he can't do the things you kids can do. Why did you let him?"

Will shook his head. "I'm sorry. I didn't know they were gonna follow me—honest."

"You had no business going up there yourself!" Tina cried. She sat up, her face scarlet and her hands wrung together like rags. "He *is* going to be fine. And he is going to *stay* fine because he is never going anywhere with you again! How many times has he been hurt or frightened because of you and your shenanigans? I'm through with it—do you hear? I'm through!"

Will watched, bewildered, as Tina threw herself back against Mom's chest. Mom looked up at him and nodded for him to step away. Her eyes were so full of worry, he couldn't tell if she was mad at him or not.

How could she not be? he thought miserably as he shoved his hands into the pockets of his dungarees and walked away from them, kicking at the dirt. *I messed this all up. She wouldn't believe me now if I told her I was just trying to protect Bud. Nobody would.*

And maybe he couldn't blame them. There was nothing to do now but wait for them to get Abe down from the mesa. It was all he could do not to climb up after them, but he was sure they wouldn't welcome his help—not if they were as angry with him as Tina was.

His mouth went dry as he dragged his toes through the dust, head down, but he barely noticed. Bud's words were all he could focus on: *You kids are like my own. If anything happened to any of you, it would be like losing Abe. I'd never be the same.*

What if Abe does die? Will thought. *It's my fault. How did I make the wrong choice? I tried so hard to guess what Jesus would want me to do—*

"Battling Boy."

Will's head snapped up. That was Quebi's name for him.

As he looked around for the owner of the voice, Will realized with a jolt that he himself was standing in the middle of the plaza, where non-Indians were forbidden to go.

"I'm sorry!" he called out. "Really—it was a mistake. I'll get off—"

"Battling Boy."

Will put his hand up to his eyebrows to block out the sun as he looked up. Watching him from the roof of his adobe house was Quebi in the usual bright blue kerchief that tied back his iron-gray hair. He nodded when Will saw him.

"Come," he said.

He motioned with a gnarled hand to a ladder which leaned against the wall. With his heart in his throat, Will climbed it. One *more* person that he loved and looked up to was disappointed in him. It was not a good day.

"I'm sorry, Quebi," Will said when he was still on the top few rungs of the ladder. "I was thinking about Abe. You heard what happened?"

Quebi nodded and shifted his eyes to the spot beside him on the roof. Will crawled to it and sat as Quebi did, with his legs folded in front of him. But unlike Quebi, Will hung his head down to his knees.

Quebi, he knew, had a walnut shell of a face that could say more with a look than most people could in 20 minutes of nonstop conversation. But Will couldn't look at it today. Quebi's all-knowing eyes would only see into him and know his shame.

"Battling Boy has burden today."

Will nodded. "It's my fault Abe got hurt. I should've just told everybody to come back down from the mesa as soon as they got there. But I didn't know what to do, Quebi! If I did one thing, it was gonna hurt Olive, and if I did the other thing, I wasn't gonna be able to help Bud. Does that make any sense? It doesn't, does it? See. I can't even say it right, so how am I ever supposed to make the right choice?"

He dropped his hands into his lap. He hadn't seen how things could get any worse, but now that he'd just made a complete fool of himself in front of Quebi, it *was* worse.

Quebi didn't say anything for a while. He'd always told Will there was wisdom in the silence.

If he's getting any wisdom, Will thought, *I sure wish he'd pass it on to me.*

Finally, he could feel Quebi looking at him, and he had to look back at him. It would be rude not to.

When his eyes met Quebi's, he was surprised to see them looking puzzled. It made his heart sink. If Quebi was confused, there was probably no hope at all.

"Why Battling Boy cannot choose?" Quebi said.

"I thought I could," Will said. "Bud told me to think about what Jesus would do if He had to make the same choice I had to; but I guess I figured wrong."

"Why?"

Will shook his head. "Because I'm an idiot."

Quebi didn't answer. There was disapproval in his silence.

"I'm sure not very smart," Will said. "There's no doubt about that."

"Not true." Quebi's eyes bored into him from over his hawkish nose. "Jesus."

He paused expectantly.

"Yeah," Will said. "Jesus."

"Jesus walk with His people as friend. Show people way to live on earth."

"Right," Will said. "That's what we believe."

Slowly Quebi's eyes widened in his wrinkled face. He turned his palm upward, as if to say, "What is the problem, then?"

"But He's not here now," Will said. "If He were, I could just walk right up to Him and ask Him."

There was another long pause, so long that Will got up on his knees to look toward the mesa to see if Dan and Bud were on their way with Abe. His stomach was in a knot, and talking to Quebi was only making it worse.

"Do so," Quebi said suddenly.

"Do what?" Will said.

"Walk with Jesus Friend."

Will could only look at him blankly. *If I knew how to do that,* he wanted to say, *I'd be doing it.*

Quebi's face grew long, and he shook his head. He looked so directly at Will, he was sure the old Indian had just read his mind.

"I don't know how to 'walk with Jesus,'" he said. "That's the problem."

"He show you."

"Jesus?"

Quebi nodded.

"But—"

"Abe Friend," Quebi said. "It is your wish he should live."

"Of course!"

"You do all. You help."

"I'd do anything for Abe. He's my friend."

Quebi cocked his head, so that the long gray curl on one side swept against his weathered cheek. "Will Friend," he said, holding up one palm. "Jesus Friend." He held up his second palm and looked from one to the other.

It was as though a shade had been raised in Will's head, letting thick shafts of sunlight slant in.

"So you're saying that . . . if Jesus is my friend, He *wants* to help me. He *wants* me to know what I'm supposed to do." Will leaned toward Quebi. "Is that what you mean?"

"Friend does not make game of trouble."

"Game. You mean like a guessing game?"

Whether Quebi would have answered, Will didn't know. There was a shout from below. It was Fawn, yelling, "Here they come! They've got Abe!"

"I gotta go," Will said, and he scrambled up and took the rungs two at a time. He knew Quebi was nodding, eyes closed, above him.

By the time Will reached the group from the mesa, Tina had already gotten to them. Her face told Will everything he needed to know. She went dead white as she looked at Abe, and the eyes she turned to Bud were stricken.

Margretta had joined them too, and she registered the same reaction to Abe's still form. "The ambulance should be here any minute," she said.

"He's breathing, and his heart is strong," Dan said. "We know for sure he has a broken leg—"

"But he's unconscious!" Tina said. "My baby is unconscious!"

Next to her, Bud wiped his hand across his eyes. Then without a word, he pulled her close to him and buried his face in her hair.

Will turned away. He couldn't watch any more.

He was sitting beside the road that led into the Pueblo when the ambulance arrived, and he walked in front of it to guide the driver to the place where Bud and Dan and the Pueblo's healer had Abe wrapped in a blanket. He watched as the attendants put his big friend onto a stretcher and loaded him into the back of the ambulance like they were delivering a washing machine.

Be careful! Will wanted to shout at them. *He's my friend.*

As the ambulance revved up its engine, Will stepped back from the road, tromping on Fawn's foot. He'd had no idea she was standing there, or Olive and Miguel either. Together they watched the ambulance disappear in its own dust with Bud and Tina following in the Chevy.

"If you guys all hate me now, I'll understand," Will said when they were gone. "I wouldn't blame you."

Three pairs of eyes, all dark, all filled with the mixture of the things they'd just seen, blinked back at him.

"Don't be a moron," Fawn said. "We're your friends."

"There is no hate, my friend," Miguel said.

But it was Olive Will looked at.

"I can't tell you—" he said.

She shook her head. "I don't care about that," she said. "We need each other."

Olive grabbed his hand. "You're stuck with us."

✢ ❖ ✢

Chapter Twelve

*T*hings began to happen fast, and the kids were all swept up in it. But knowing they were still his friends kept Will from folding up in his own misery several times during the next few hours.

Abe was taken to St. Vincent's Hospital, and by the time Mom and Margretta and Dan and Conchita and the four kids arrived, the doctors had already told Tina and Bud that Abe had not only a broken leg but had suffered a severe concussion and probably some internal injuries as well.

"What does 'internal injuries' mean?" Fawn whispered to Will.

Will wasn't sure, but from the way Tina buried her face in her hands, he knew it couldn't be good.

Everyone gathered in the waiting room except Tina, who insisted on standing just outside the emergency room door so she could pounce on every doctor, nurse, and orderly who came out. Will was secretly glad she was pouncing on them and not him, but that made him feel guilty.

She should *be all over me,* he thought as he sat sighing in a hard metal chair. *It's my fault.*

It was worse to look across the waiting room at Bud, who was standing at the window, staring out. Will knew he wasn't seeing Santa

Fe; he was seeing big, lovable Abe, the kid he'd waited so long to get.

God? Will prayed over and over. *Please—Abe has to be okay, even if I made a bad choice. Please don't make Abe be the one to get punished. Please. He can't even make his own choices—*

The thought was too much. Will got up and stood in the doorway, so that he was halfway between Tina and the rest of the group. When the emergency room door opened, he could hear the words of the doctor who tried to step through and was accosted by Tina.

"He's going to need surgery," the doctor said. "First so we can try to stop the bleeding in his abdomen, then when he's strong enough we'll go back in and work on that leg."

Tina turned to Bud, who had stumbled over several people to get to her. Her face crumpled.

"What's an 'abdomen'?" Fawn whispered from behind Will.

They all watched two men in white uniforms wheel Abe out of the emergency room and down the hall toward the operating room. He was covered with a white sheet, and only his still-bluish face and his big feet were showing.

Will wanted to run to him, to tell him once more that he was sorry, that it was going to be all right. He even started to step forward, but two things stopped him.

Miguel grabbing his arm.

And Bud looking up at him—and shaking his head. His eyes were cold, and they took Will's breath away.

Bud and Tina followed Abe to the operating room area, where, the nurse told them, there was another waiting room. Margretta went with them, and Will started to follow, but this time it was Mom who stopped him.

"The rest of us are going home," she said. "We'll wait at our house for news."

Will felt as if he were tearing off an arm, leaving Abe there. He was the last one to straggle out of the hospital and get in the car.

"It's not all your fault, you know," Olive whispered to him as he squeezed into the backseat between her and Miguel. "You have to stop thinking that."

But all the way back to Canyon Road, as Mom and Dan and Conchita talked in quiet voices in the front seat, that was all he could think. He could still see Bud's eyes, stone cold and hard as he let Will know he didn't want him to be with his son—not now—maybe not ever.

He's so disappointed in me, he thought. *I don't think I can stand it*.

The hardest part, he decided as Mom pulled Margretta's car into the driveway, was that he'd been up on the mesa in the first place to *help* Bud.

And now I can't do that—

Or can't I? Can't I find some way—some safe way—to help him, so he'll know? So he'll trust me again?

But the minute he got out of the car, he knew that was hopeless. In the first place, Mr. T. and Señora Otero were there to meet them, both looking anxious—and disappointed. And before Will could even point himself in their direction, to try to explain to yet two more people he respected that he wasn't a complete idiot, Mom caught him by the arm.

"You kids go upstairs," she said. "The adults need to talk."

"Mom . . . I—"

"Go, Will," she said. "We're all too tired to argue."

Fawn was the first one up the stairs once they got inside. She was never one to cross Mama Hutchie. But Will dragged behind. He felt so heavy, each step was an effort. He'd only gotten about halfway up when he heard Dan's voice from the living room where the adults were gathered.

"I'm going to make a suggestion, and I know it's going to seem outlandish to you, so just hear me out."

"If you're going to suggest we string them all up by their thumbs, I'm all for it," Mom said. "What on earth were they thinking?"

Not they, Will wanted to tell her. *Just me—*

He could hear Mr. T. clearing his throat. "I hesitate to put my two cents in," he said, "since none of these are my own children, though I am legally responsible for Olive—"

"Please, put your two cents in," Mom said. "Put a whole dollar in. I need all the help I can get."

"Amen to that," Dan said.

Will could feel Fawn and Olive and Miguel creeping back down the stairs behind him.

"What's going on?" Olive whispered.

Will put his finger to his lips. They all crammed together like a pile of puppies and listened.

"There will need to be consequences," Mr. T. was saying, "though I think stringing them up by their thumbs might be a little extreme."

"Whew," Fawn whispered.

"Their behavior was irresponsible and they need to learn from it," Mr. T. went on.

"I gotta go down there," Will whispered.

"Are you nuts?" Fawn whispered back.

"They only need to punish *me*. I gotta tell them that."

Will tried to get up, but Fawn grabbed him around the neck from behind, and Olive stopped him with a firm, whispered, "No!"

It was suddenly quiet in the living room, and for an awful moment Will thought they had all heard the whispering. But then Señora Otero said, "We have seen them behave this way before—"

"Exactly my point," Mom said.

"But there is always a reason."

There was another silence. Will could hear his own pulse.

"You have a point there," Mr. T. said finally. "Though for the life of me I can't fathom what it might be this time."

"Then we should ask them," Mom said.

Will slapped his hand over his mouth so he wouldn't shout, "No!"

"After all we've been through with these kids," Mr. T. said, "I'm pretty sure if they wanted us to know what they were thinking, they would have told us. Heaven knows they have enough mentors who are willing to listen to them."

"What's a 'mentor'?" Fawn whispered.

Olive pointed toward the living room. "All of them," she whispered.

"Well, like I said, I have a suggestion," Dan said. "It's going to sound ridiculous at first, but if you'll just hear me out—"

"It can't be any more ridiculous than my idea," Mom said.

There was a little shuffling around, and Will guessed everyone was turning to look at Dan. It gave Will a chance to do some shuffling of his own, to get Fawn off of his neck. She let go, but not before holding up a warning finger.

"I saw desperation in what they did today," Dan said.

"What's 'desper'—"

All three of the kids turned on Fawn with their fingers on their lips.

"Think about it," Dan went on. "They've had their riding privileges all but taken away—by their own doing. So I think their hike up the mesa was an attempt to regain some of that freedom."

"So they're desperate for freedom?" Mom said. "Aren't we all?"

"But desperate for the freedom to do or find some particular thing. I don't think it's just their wanting to get away from all of us."

As Dan paused, Will turned to his friends to stare. They were already staring back.

"So why haven't they come to us?" Mr. T. said. "Will knows he can talk to me about anything. Olive, too."

"That's what I think we have to find out," Dan said.

"Let me get them down here," Mom said.

"Well, maybe we should wait, Ingrid," Mr. T. said.

Will looked at Olive. She was mouthing a "thank you."

"I want to hear Dan's idea," Mr. T. said. "I'm intrigued."

"Yes," Señora Otero put in. "I am as well."

"Here's my plan," Dan said. "Why don't I take all four of them on an overnight camping trip with the horses? They'll have a little bit of their freedom, but they won't be without an adult, and I'll have time to spend listening to them until I find out what they're after."

Will could feel his eyes popping. Olive put her hand over Fawn's mouth so she wouldn't blurt out something. Even Miguel looked ready to jump.

"But isn't that rewarding them for irresponsible behavior?" Mom said.

"Why don't they just speak English?" Fawn whispered through Olive's fingers.

"I'm not suggesting that we don't each give our own child a punishment," Dan said. "But I think this could get us to the root of the problem."

"I see your point." That came from Mr. T. Will squeezed his eyes shut and prayed that his mother would "see" it too.

"What about you ladies?" Mom said. "Do you think this could work?"

"Fawn—she is not as I was," Conchita said.

That's for sure, Will thought. He almost grinned at Fawn.

"I cannot tell. I go with Daniel."

"I don't have anybody to 'go' with," Mom said.

A pang went through Will. He was making things harder for Mom when she had it bad enough to begin with.

"Nor do I, Ingrid," Señora Otero was saying. "I know that Miguel looks up to Will as if he were a brother. If I say no—if I say he cannot be with his friend—I am taking away yet another thing that is important in his life."

Another pang hit Will—a sharper, guiltier pang this time. Was there even one person that meant something to him who he wasn't hurting right now?

Jesus! he prayed. *Please be my friend and walk with me—and show me! Please!*

"All right, Dan," Mom said out of the quiet that had fallen below. "Let's give it a try. But before you take them on this trip, Will is going to be doing some serious penance around here."

"Atta girl, Ingrid," Mr. T. said, his dry laugh crackling through. "Give it to him with both barrels."

"What do you think she'll do to you?" Olive whispered.

Will shook his head. He really didn't care. Nothing would be too bad for what he'd allowed to happen to Abe. The real punishment was going to be having Dan try to get him to talk about his quest—and not being able to tell him a thing.

"I'd really like to pray about this," Mom said from below. "Do you mind if we—"

"Mind? I'd love to," Dan said.

"See?" Fawn whispered. "My dad really is a Christian now."

Miguel smiled and patted her on the shoulder. Olive leaned her head to listen and then turned to the group. "While they're praying," she said almost soundlessly, "we should get back up to Will's room—"

But the rest of the sentence fell silent on her lips. They were hit by a sudden shaft of light which shot down the stairs and exposed the four of them huddled there.

Fawn barely got her hand over her mouth in time to stifle a scream, and even Olive gave a start. But Will knew exactly what it was, and his heart sank like a stone.

It was Aunt Hildy Helen, emerging from the attic. She stopped, folded her arms across her chest, and simply stared.

"Uh-oh," Olive whispered.

"Yeah," Will whispered back. "Uh-oh."

✝ ◆ ✝

Chapter Thirteen

There was no choice this time, as far as Will was concerned. There was only one thing to do, and that was to keep Aunt Hildy Helen from telling Mom that they'd been eavesdropping. And there was only one way to do it.

Will stood up and, turning to his aunt, put his finger to his lips. Then he pointed to the attic. Miguel, Olive, and Fawn got to their feet and padded up the steps, passing Aunt Hildy on their way in.

"We have to be quiet," Will whispered to her. "They're praying down there."

Aunt Hildy looked down the steps, a puzzled expression on her face.

"They really are," Will whispered. "They do it all the time."

To his surprise, and relief, Aunt Hildy just shrugged. She started toward the steps then, but Will got himself in front of her.

"My friends want to see our family tree," he whispered. "Will you show us?"

It was only partly a lie. He knew they *would* want to see it, once they found out that was the best way to distract Aunt Hildy from spilling the beans to Mom.

Aunt Hildy gave a tired sigh and nodded. Will held the door for her like the perfect gentleman, though his real motive was to make sure she went in and didn't go down the stairs once his back was turned.

I still have to remember that she's a little sick in her head, Will told himself.

Inside the attic, Miguel, Olive, and Fawn were huddled together and looking at him blankly. Will let his voice go slightly above a whisper as he said, "I told Aunt Hildy we wanted to see the family tree she's doing."

"Oh," Olive said. "Yeah."

"What's a family tree?" Fawn said.

This time it was Miguel who clapped his hand over her mouth. Aunt Hildy Helen didn't seem to notice.

"There it is," Hildy said, panning the paper with her flashlight.

"Wow," Olive said. "There sure have been a lot of Hutchinsons."

"There have," Hildy said. "And now most of them are dead."

Fawn blinked at her. Miguel and Olive looked at each other. Will felt a little sick.

"Well, they would be, wouldn't they?" Olive said. She pointed to the top branch. "These people—John and Deborah—they lived back in the 1600s. Of course they'd be dead."

"Exactly my point," Aunt Hildy Helen said. It was probably the most Will had heard her talk, but she was still using that flat voice that sounded like it, too, was "dead."

"You're born," she went on, "and then you die."

Fawn's brow puckered. "But isn't there stuff in between?" she said.

"Does it matter?" Aunt Hildy said.

"I sure hope so!" Olive said. She cocked an eyebrow at Will. He knew she'd already figured out that something wasn't quite right with Aunt Hildy Helen.

Fawn, on the other hand, was still trying to make sense of it all. She pointed to some writing on the paper which hadn't been there when Will had last seen it.

"What's this?" she said.

"I'm writing in their occupations," Aunt Hildy said.

"Their what?"

"Their jobs," Miguel said.

"I thought it would tell me why they bothered living," Aunt Hildy said.

Will looked around the attic. He wasn't sure what he expected to see, but there was a cold, dark feeling in there which he had never felt before. The whole conversation was making his stomach knot up. Maybe it would have been better to just let Aunt Hildy tell Mom she'd discovered them on the steps.

"They did a little bit of everything, those Hutchinsons," Olive said. She traced her finger down the tree. "Farmer. Ship captain. Shipping merchant. Doctor. Abolitionist—"

Olive stopped and grinned at Fawn. "Even I don't know what an abolitionist is."

"He was against slavery," Hildy Helen said.

"Then I am an abolitionist, as well," Miguel said.

His eyes were kind as he nodded at Aunt Hildy. She looked at him for a moment before she went back to the paper. "This is my father," she said, pointing to the name James Rudolph Hutchinson. "He was an attorney, like his father before him."

"A lawyer," Olive said to Fawn.

"What about the girls?" Fawn said. "Didn't they have occu—those job things?"

Hildy nodded. "My Great-Aunt Gussie worked for women to get the vote."

"She knew Margretta Dietrich back then," Will put in.

"Sally Hutchinson worked alongside her husband, the abolitionist. Virginia Hutchinson organized the women in Williamsburg to aid the soldiers in the American Revolution—" Hildy stopped. The light that had come into her eyes faded, and her face hardened flat again. "Silly woman," she said. "She actually thought war accomplished something."

Will froze. This was not the conversation he wanted to get into. Not only did it send Aunt Hildy Helen back into her dark corner, but

it was obviously stabbing Miguel right in the heart. He expected Fawn
to jump the woman, when Olive spoke up.

"Huh," she said. "You sound just like my father. You should talk
to him."

That would be a party, Will thought. *Maybe they could get every-body else at the sanitarium to join in.*

"Who's your father?" Aunt Hildy Helen said.

"He's a conscientious objector," Olive said. "Only it's made him
sick."

Hildy Helen nodded. "It makes me sick too." She paused and
swept her eyes over the family tree. "Maybe I'll just pay him a visit."

Before Will could open his mouth to say that wasn't a good idea,
Olive said, "His name's Eduardo Fernandez. He's in St. Vincent's—in
the sanitarium part."

"I know the place," Aunt Hildy said. "They wanted to put me
there too. I came here instead."

Do you have *to tell all my friends you're almost a crazy person?*
Will thought.

But Miguel was still looking at her with his kind eyes, and Fawn
was too fascinated by the family tree to even let it sink in. Olive was
nodding as if she and Aunt Hildy were having an intelligent
conversation.

"You're lucky to be here with Ingrid and Will," Olive said. "If I
weren't with Mr. T. and Señora Otero, this is where I'd want to be."

"Why?" Aunt Hildy Helen said.

"It's the food," Will said quickly. "You know what a great cook
Mom is."

"No, Will," Olive said. She turned to Hildy Helen. "It's the hope,"
she said. "They never give up in this house."

"Will? Where have you gotten to now?"

That was Mom's voice, calling from the bottom of the stairs. Will
lunged for the door with the other three behind him. It was too late
to worry anymore about Aunt Hildy.

But as he flung open the door and yelled down, "We're up here,

Mom!" he heard his aunt say to Olive, "Hey, don't worry. Your secret's safe with me."

The camping trip was set for mid-July, which gave the kids two weeks to get ready, and Mom just as long to lower the boom on Will. She couldn't seem to make up her mind what punishment to give him, and so it loomed in the future like a dreaded dentist appointment.

Although he loved sitting down with Dan and the others and planning what food they would take and what equipment they would need to put in their saddlebags, it was hard to keep up his excitement when he was alone. It wasn't just the unknown punishment that clouded his thoughts. It was Abe.

The day after the accident, Mom took Will to St. Vincent's to see him. Olive went along so she could visit her father. Why she should want to do that was beyond Will.

"I don't get it," he told his mother as Olive hurried down the stairs at the hospital. "If I was Olive, I'd be afraid he'd clobber me or something."

"Eduardo isn't violent," Mom said. "As a matter of fact, he's a very sensitive, high-strung person. Too much so—so that sometimes he goes over the edge. But he doesn't want to hurt anybody—I think that's the whole point. He's so angry about the war because of all the death it's causing."

Will shivered. He really didn't want to talk about that. And besides, as he walked down the hall with Mom, he saw Tina, guarding Abe's door like a German shepherd. When she saw Will, she all but bared her teeth at him, and all thoughts of Eduardo and war left his head.

"He can't have visitors," Tina said—with a snarl.

"Of course we wouldn't want to disturb him," Mom said. "We just wanted to show our concern."

"Why can't he have visitors?" Will said.

Mom gave him a soft nudge with her elbow, but Will ignored it. His fear was too raw for him to think about manners. He had to know.

"Because he's still unconscious," Tina said.

"From the surgery?" Mom said.

"No—from his head injuries." Tina looked straight at Will. "They're saying he may never wake up at all."

"You mean—he'll die?" Will said.

"Or worse—slip into a coma and lie there for the rest of his days. The boy who loved life more than anyone—"

Tina choked on her own voice. Mom tried to put her arm around her but she pulled away and retreated into Abe's room, snapping the door shut behind her. Will felt her words scrape over his already raw feelings. He knew if he cried, he would never be able to stop.

"Oh, Son," Mom said. She put both arms around him and pulled him close to her. He didn't care that the hall was filled with staring people. He let his face fall into her shoulder.

"I know I told you that you were irresponsible to go up on that mesa without telling anyone, but, Son, this was not all your fault. Olive and Fawn brought him up there, uninvited. Tina put you children in charge of Abe, and that was asking too much. The girls couldn't pick him up and carry him back to his mother when he refused to stay behind, like they would a small child—and yet he *is* a child in his mind. It is too much to expect kids to always know how to handle that."

Will pulled away from her to look into her face. "He trusted me, and he made the same choice just because I did."

Mom opened her mouth, and Will knew it was to ask him why— why he had made that choice. But instead, she pressed her lips together.

"I just want to see Abe, Mom," Will said. "I know he's unconscious and he *probably* can't hear me, but *maybe* he can. I just wanna tell him I'm sorry."

"I don't know, Will," Mom said.

"I do," a voice said.

Will turned sharply. It was Bud, standing a few feet from them with a large stuffed teddy bear under his arm.

Will searched his face—looked at his eyes—and his heart

dropped. Bud's eyes were puffy, with lines at their corners extending out in a network of sleeplessness. They were no longer cold and hard, but they didn't welcome Will, either.

"This isn't a good time for you to see Abe," he said.

"I know Tina's mad at me," Will said. "But, Bud, if you'd just—"

"Will—would it be so hard for you to just listen to somebody and do what they say?"

Will stared. Bud's eyes grew moist around the edges, and his pudgy lips shook, just as his voice did. "You can't see Abe right now," he said. He let himself into the hospital room. The closing of the door echoed in the hall.

"Come on, Son," Mom said. "Let's go home."

Will trailed his mother down the hall and around the corner toward the front door, lagging behind so he wouldn't have to talk. A voice hissed at him from the direction of the stairwell. It was Olive, beckoning him with her finger.

"Mom," Will said. "I'm gonna go up and wait for Olive."

"Sure," Mom said. "I'll sit out there on the steps."

Will watched her go through the front door and felt one of his biggest pangs yet. She looked so sad, and it occurred to him for the first time that, of course, she would be. Abe had lived with them for a short time, and he had called her "Mutti," the German name for mother. Like Bud, she loved all the kids as if they were her own. She was grieving for Abe, just like Will was.

Will turned to Olive to tell her that he'd better go out and sit with his mom, but her face stopped him. Something was very wrong.

He slipped through the door into the stairwell. Olive started to talk before it even sighed shut behind him.

"That lady—the one with the Jeep—" she said.

"Up at Los Alamos?" Will said.

"Yeah. Will, she's here!"

"She's in the hospital? She's a patient?"

"No. She's visiting."

"So?"

Olive put her face close to his. "She's visiting my dad!"

All Will could do was blink at her.

"I don't know how she knows him or anything," Olive went on. "I just asked the nurse if I could go in and see him and she said he could only have one visitor at a time and there was already somebody in there, so I looked through the window in his door and there she was, talking away to him like they were old friends or something."

"How do you know it was the same lady?"

"I'll never forget that face—will you?"

Will shook his head. She'd had a red gash for a mouth. You didn't forget something like that.

"Plus she was wearing the same dress she had on the second time we saw her."

"How would you remember that?"

"Because I'm a girl, Einstein! And get this—"

"What?"

"She had a red hibiscus blossom tucked behind her ear."

"So do you think . . ."

Will let his voice fade. Olive was nodding.

"The woman at the Los Alamos gate and the woman who's visiting my father and the woman that FBI guy was looking at that day at LaFonda are all the same person." Olive folded her arms and leaned against the stairwell wall. "What on earth could my father possibly have to do with Los Alamos? The only time he ever leaves here is when he's with me on a pass. As far as I know, he only has one friend here—some guy who's as off his beam about the war as Dad is. What do you think's going on?"

"Gee, I don't know," Will said. He tried to make his voice sound curious, but he wasn't sure he was pulling it off. He carefully studied the toe of his shoe. Eduardo Fernandez's argument with Bud the night of the wedding echoed in his ears.

Olive sighed. "I guess we'd better go if you and your mom are finished here. I'll come back and see my dad tomorrow." She looked closely at Will. "Did you get to see Abe?"

Will shook his head. "Looks like we both struck out," he said.

Over the next 10 days, the only thing that kept Will from retreating to the attic like Aunt Hildy Helen was the promise of the camping trip. News that President Truman was going to Potsdam in Germany to meet with leaders from Britain and the Soviet Union to demand Japan's unconditional surrender didn't cheer him up. Word from Margretta that she had been back to the Pueblo and Quebi had been asking about him didn't improve his mood. Even a surprise phone call from Uncle Al, checking in on his family, didn't give him hope. Abe was still unconscious, Tina wouldn't let Will in to see him, and Bud was too disappointed in him to even talk to him in the hallway. Will stopped going to the hospital at all. As for what Olive had discovered about Hibiscus Lady, he didn't even want to think about that. He couldn't help Bud, and even if he could it would only mean heartache for Olive.

He was in an especially dark place in his mind a few nights before the trip when Mom came into his room and sat on his bed.

"I've decided on your punishment," she said.

Will nodded. "I know what it is: You're not going to let me go on the trip, right?"

Mom pulled her head back to look at him.

"I'd hate it," Will said. "But I'd understand why you had to do it. I don't deserve to go."

"Will—what on *earth?*" Mom said. "You made a mistake, but that doesn't mean you don't deserve another minute of happiness your whole life."

Will just shrugged.

"Well, that isn't your punishment," she said. "In fact, it isn't really a punishment at all. I think you're piling enough suffering on yourself. It's more of a way to teach you something—that's what a good punishment should do anyway."

"Mom, why don't you just beat me and get it over with?" Will said.

She actually laughed. "And when have I ever beaten you, Will Hutchinson?"

"I never did anything this bad before."

Mom stood up and crooked her finger at him. "Come with me," she said.

He followed her down to the kitchen, sure that she was going to make him do a whole day's worth of dishes. But the sink was clean, and she pointed to his chair at the table.

"Sit," she said.

"Do I have to peel potatoes?" he said. "I'll do it. I won't even complain—"

"We already had supper," Mom said, her mouth twitching. "How soon they forget. Hildy? Could you come in here for a minute, please?"

"Mo-om," Will said under his breath.

She ignored him and ushered Aunt Hildy Helen into the room. Will hadn't had a conversation with her since the night of the accident, which was fine with him. Although she had opened up some that night with Olive, from what he could tell she had gone back into her cave since then. Even now, she sat at the table and looked down at her hands.

"Coffee?" Mom said.

She shook her head.

"Streusel?"

"No, thank you."

She offered some to Will, but he refused too. He knew it would only turn to sawdust in his mouth.

Mom sat at the table with them. "Hildy, Will is still feeling like Abe's accident is all his fault, because he made a poor choice."

Hildy Helen said nothing, which didn't surprise Will.

"So I was thinking," Mom went on, "that you could tell him about some of the mistakes you kids made when you were growing up—you and Rudy and Al. I'd like him to see that you learned from your mistakes—that you didn't drag them around with you for the rest of your lives."

Aunt Hildy shrugged. Will stared at the side of his mother's face. Did she really think Aunt Hildy Helen was going to burst into childhood tales when she'd barely spoken a complete sentence the whole time she'd been there?

"What about the time you and Rudy took Aunt Gussie's parrot down to Greektown to try to scare those thugs? What was that bird's name?"

"Picasso," Aunt Hildy said.

"Right. It was the smartest bird I ever saw, and you and Rudy almost lost the thing. Tell Will about that."

"You just did," Hildy said.

"Oh. Okay, what about the night the three of you got tied up in that old warehouse? That was a huge mistake, but you all learned from it—"

"And what good did it do us?" Hildy Helen said.

Her voice was so filled-up and strong, Will sat back in his chair.

"Rudy is in a concentration camp. Al is heaven knows where. And I can barely put two thoughts together. So what good did anything we learned do us? The war came along and ruined everything. For everyone."

With a scrape of her chair across the tile, Aunt Hildy Helen was up and out of the room. Will and his mother sat in stunned silence as they listened to her footsteps, stomping all the way up to the attic.

"Poor thing," Mom said when they heard the door close.

"What happened to her?" Will said.

"Just like she said—the war."

"Is Dad gonna be like that when he gets home?"

"No."

"But how do you know?"

Mom turned so that she could look Will straight in the eyes. "Because he will *choose* not to, that's how I know. He's praying to God every day to help him hang on and not give up—I know he is. That's the choice he would want you to make too, Will. And you know it."

Will couldn't sleep for a long time that night. Every time he closed his eyes, he could see his father praying in some cold, dark place, asking God for hanging-on help.

I guess he doesn't have any choices at all, he thought. *That's all he can do.*

He curled up in a ball and ached for his dad.

For the next two days Will helped pack the food sacks and groom the horses and plan out the route with Dan.

"So which way do you want to go?" Dan said. "We could head west over to Bandalier and see the ancient Anasazi ruins, or we could go south to Cerrillos and see some turquoise country—"

"We've already done that, thank you," Olive said.

"Or we could head north," Dan said.

Will could feel his friends holding their breath. Dan himself just waited. It was Will's choice—at last.

Your father would want you to choose to hang on and not give up, his mother had said. *Jesus Friend wants you to know what to do,* Quebi had said. *Jesus speaks to us through wise people,* Bud had told him.

"What do you think?" Will said.

"I think north is a good plan," Dan said.

Will nodded. "Then north it is."

✠ ⋅✠⋅ ✠

Chapter Fourteen

They left early the next morning, July 15, from Mr. T.'s ranch, waving to Mom and Señora Otero and Conchita as Mr. T. opened the gate to let them pass through.

"Take care of my horses," he said to Dan and Olive, who were riding two of his mares, while Will and Miguel and Fawn rode Señora Otero's horses, as always.

"Don't worry," Olive said. "I have it all under control."

"That's what I'm afraid of," Mr. T. said.

But his smile flashed, and Will knew things were getting back to normal with him. He tried to brush the thought of Bud away and focused himself on Cisco and the road ahead.

"Will!" his mother called to him.

Will turned to see her standing on the lowest slat of the fence. Her eyes were shiny, and Will thought he could see tears in them.

"Just remember what I told you," she said.

"I remember," Will said.

"What did she tell you?" Olive asked him when the ranch was no more than a collection of specks behind them.

"She told me to hang on and not give up," he said.

"Oh," Olive said. "I thought you always did that."

At first it was hard for Will to leave Santa Fe behind in his mind. Tina and Abe seemed to be in every piñon and cedar and cactus, reminding him of his bad choices. Eduardo Fernandez and Agent Graves and Hibiscus Lady were in the grasshoppers that flicked from the ground sounding like electrical shorts, tempting him to find out more.

But it was Bud he saw the most, watching him in the face of every deer and jackrabbit and blue-tailed lizard they startled along the way. *Don't disappoint me again,* they seemed to say. *Don't hurt my children anymore.*

Yet as the day went on and they traveled farther from town and into the secret places in the desert and the hills, it was hard for Will not to begin to feel the peace that was there waiting for them.

In some places the ground was a splurge of wildflowers—the scarlet gilia, the red and orange Indian paintbrush and yarrow, waving in the breeze like wands or twining around rocks or overflowing in terraces of color. Even the black-eyed Susans caught his eye as they hadn't before. Where once they'd just been weeds, they now seemed wild and tall like lanky adolescent girls. Like Fawn.

In other places the rocks entranced him, looming castlelike on the ridge above them as they rode. Some were tinted shades of pink by the sun; others were rich with reds and rusts. Still more were so bleached-white they made Will squint. It was easy to see why the Indians used the colors they did to make their pottery and blankets.

Will had decided the rocks were his favorite when Miguel pointed out the birds. He got a crick in his neck from following first the path of a black hawk across the sky, then a pair of eagles going to and from a lofty nest, their white-tipped wings and white heads shining in the sun.

By noon the group had left the softer rolling hills and were starting into layered rock. It grew cooler as they climbed, even in July, and Will saw the chill in Olive and Miguel's cheeks. Fawn seemed made for the weather, and she rode next to her father, sitting straight in the saddle with her arms bare to the wind, just like his. It sent a pang of envy through Will—a pang that made him think, *I'm choos-*

ing to hang on, Dad. I'm hanging on 'til you come home. Maybe it was the only choice *he* had too.

After they ate lunch—Señora Otero's tamales which she'd wrapped for them in waxed paper—Dan suggested that they let the horses rest in the shade while they explored some of the caves.

"I don't know if that's such a good idea," Will said. He looked up at the rock wall, punched in with "rooms." "What if somebody falls?"

"We can't live our lives in fear of 'what if,' " Dan said.

"Abe fell."

"We will be careful," Dan said.

Fawn had already ascended like a monkey to the first cave, which was scooped out of the side of the mountain, and she sat there swinging her legs. "I like it up here!" she called down. "Come on, everyone! Start climbing!"

"Thanks just the same," Olive said. "But I'd hate to see this path go to waste."

She motioned to the boys, and the three of them started up a narrow trail that twisted its way to the caves.

"Chickens!" Fawn called down.

"Smart chickens," Olive called up.

Fawn watched them for a minute and then popped off of her perch to join them. Obviously, it looked like more fun than being better and faster.

As they followed the curving path, the rock formations seemed to Will to come alive, as though they were calling up to the heavens or looking down on them like great frogs. Even rocks that tilted toward them from the side of the mountain seemed to protect them rather than threaten to fall on them.

It's like God's holding them up, Will thought.

"See how it sparkles," Miguel said, pointing to the speckled glints of sunlight on the rocks.

"See how it crumbles off in your hand when you touch it," Olive said dryly. She showed her white, sandy palm to Dan. "Should we be worried about that?"

"I don't think the Indians who lived here a couple of thousand years ago worried about it," Dan said.

"Then these caves were their houses?" Miguel said.

"They were."

"I wanna live up here!" Fawn said. "Look how fun!" She slithered easily through a narrow passageway in the twisting path where rocks came up to meet them on either side.

Will climbed over the rocks and used the pockmarks in the wall as handholds to get himself to a small cave-room. A black, furry caterpillar in the entrance lifted its head to look at Will and then continued on its way, as if he didn't mind Will coming in. Will crawled carefully over it and turned to sit in the smooth cup of a room, and when he did, he decided Fawn was right. He wanted to live up there too.

The only sounds he heard in the big silence were happy ones—crickets cheerfully chirping, *Fawn* cheerfully chirping! And from the entrance to the cave there was nothing to see that wasn't beautiful: endless mountains, deep-cut canyons, gatherings of white birches whose leaves sparkled like coins, the Pajarito River winding below, a narrow blue ribbon.

"How could anyone look at this and not believe in a Power greater than themselves?" said a low voice nearby.

It didn't startle Will. Dan's voice seemed to somehow fit with the perfect quiet of the place.

"You mean God?" Will said.

"I think my people—and your people—have always known God."

Will couldn't see his face as he stood leaning on the rock wall below him, but he guessed he was smiling.

"We haven't always *listened* to God, mind you," Dan said, "but we've known He is there."

"How do you listen?" Will said. "I mean, you personally."

"I get to a quiet place, just like you're doing."

They didn't say anything for a while. Olive and Miguel and Fawn were laughing down the path, making it easier for Will to be comfortable with his thoughts.

"Quebi says he thinks Jesus wants us to know what He wants us to do," he said finally. "He says Jesus isn't playing some guessing game—He makes it clear."

"Quebi's right. I can't tell you *how* Jesus does it. I just know I've felt that. It's why I knew I had to make my marriage to Conchita right before God. It's why I knew I should let Fawn stay in Santa Fe a while longer with her friends. It's why I knew I should bring you kids up here."

So you could find out what we're up to, Will wanted to say.

There was a time, he knew, when he would have blurted that right out. But he didn't see the point in it now. For one thing, they weren't really "up to" anything right now. And for another, it might spoil this moment, and Will didn't want that. It was a moment he wanted to take a picture of and save in his scrapbook and show his dad when he came home—

"I don't really know much about this area," Dan was saying. "I do know that's the Pajarito Plateau—that one with all the canyons slashed in it—"

"Which one?" Will said. He tried not to let his voice sound too interested, but he was already sitting straight up, straining to see.

"That big one right there," Dan said.

Will leaned over to watch him point. The plateau was the very next one they would come to if they kept riding.

"Can we get to it today?" Will said.

Dan shook his head. "I think we're nearly done for today," he said. "Do you hear that?"

Will listened. A moment later, thunder rumbled in the distance like a faraway threat.

"We have a storm coming in," Dan said.

"Are you sure it's thunder?" Will said. "Or is it one of those other things?"

"What things?"

"Those things that have been shaking the ground all summer."

"Ah." Dan tilted his head as Will climbed down from his cave. "That's thunder all right," he said. "You can see the storm—look."

Will joined him on the path, and together they leaned on the chest-high rock wall to survey the sky over the mountains. Dark, heavy clouds were gathering at their peaks, and even as they watched, lightning flickered.

"The wind is going to pick up at the front of that," Dan said. "If we rode over there this afternoon, we'd go right into the storm. Can't you feel it on your skin?"

The air did have a different feel, almost as though it were charged with anticipation. Still, Will was disappointed. Los Alamos couldn't be more than 10 miles away from this very spot.

"But it just seems like the storm's so far away," Will said. "I mean, even though you can feel it."

"I think of the war that way."

Will looked up to find Dan watching him closely.

"The war?" Will said.

"Yeah. It's very far away. We don't think it can hurt us here. But we can still feel it."

For a long moment, Will couldn't tear his eyes away from Dan's. He knew with every second that went by he was giving information away, but he couldn't help it. Dan was studying him—and it didn't feel like a bad thing at all. Bud had said Jesus spoke through wise people . . .

But I can't drag anybody else into this, Will told himself firmly. *I've gotten enough people hurt already.*

As the canopy of clouds continued to move its black self toward them, Dan quickly gathered the other kids, and the group made its hurried way on horseback to a spot farther up from the canyon floor.

"We'll be safe from flash floods up here," Dan said. "This is an inviting place, don't you think?"

As they set up their tents, fighting the wind that flapped the canvas, the pines tossed their branches in the howling wind. Thunder threatened from the mountains that if they didn't button things up, they would be blown away. The horses whinnied nervously as if to say, "Don't you think you should be getting us to the stables about now?"

Will could hear it all "talking." He didn't have to see the lightning as it gashed the sky, top to bottom, to know that this was going to be a treacherous storm.

"Should we do something?" Will said. The first big drops were already clinging to the pine needles.

"Don't smile," Dan said. "The wind will hurt your front teeth."

"He's right!" Fawn said, grinning.

"And I'd say now would be a good time to hunker down in our tents."

"Separate tents?" Olive said, glancing anxiously at the sky.

"My tent," Dan said.

They all crowded into Dan's teepee of a tent just as the big drops broke through the pines and pattered against the ground. Although the wind picked up the flap and waved it like a furious flag, the tent remained sturdy and the kids were soon able to forget the storm and listen to Dan's tales of his adventures at war. They were fun things— like the night he'd been mistaken for a Japanese soldier in the middle of Germany and taken prisoner by an American unit.

He was just winding down that story when the storm finished blowing its way through and went on down the canyon. Olive, Miguel, and Fawn had all fallen asleep in a pile. Dan pulled blankets over them and motioned for Will to follow him outside.

They checked the stream, which was barely swollen, and built a small fire. Will remembered that Quebi always made a fire small, so that people could get close to it, rather than making it huge so that they had to stand away from it and let their backs grow cold.

"This trip has already been a success for me," Dan said after the long silence that always followed the first flames of a campfire.

"It has?" Will said.

"I've decided what I want to do with my life." He smiled into the fire. "When I was in Europe, it seemed impossible to think of anything else but winning the war and staying alive. Now that I'm here, with Fawn and all of you, I see what she's been doing, and I know that's the purpose of my life."

"No offense," Will said, "but I don't get it."

"I've seen how Fawn has become completely comfortable in the white man's society. She'll do well—she has friends—she knows what's good in Anglos. But she has also been drawn back to her own people, and she won't give up the best of her traditions."

"Like the stuff Quebi teaches," Will said.

"Exactly. I want to teach my Indian brothers and sisters how to do what she's done." Dan's eyes glittered clear in the firelight. "It's good to know your direction. I've found it up here in the quiet where I can listen." He looked at Will. "How about you, my friend? Have you found what you've come up here looking for?"

Will could feel his eyes springing open. If was as if Dan had lulled him to sleep and then suddenly awakened him with a poke in the side.

And yet it wasn't a nosy poke. It was a friendly one. It was a nudge that said, *I'm your friend. You can trust me with your secret.*

But it's not just my secret! Will wanted to tell him. *That's the part that makes me still not know what to do but hang on!*

Dan was once again gazing at the flames that licked at the wood, but Will wanted him to look at him. Even in the warmth of the fire, even with Dan right there beside him, he suddenly felt cold and alone with his thoughts.

"I want to tell you," Will said. "It's about a choice I gotta make—only it's about Bud—and maybe Olive. If I tell—they could maybe get hurt."

Dan nodded. There wasn't a trace of isn't-that-cute in his eyes. "You're a good friend," he said.

Will grunted.

"Do you want to be a better one?"

"What do you mean?" Will said.

"Tell *them* about this decision you have to make. Don't they have a voice in it if it affects them?"

Will considered that in the dancing fire flames. "I just thought I could save them getting hurt any more. You know, Olive's already got a crazy . . . well, what do you guys call him?"

"Disturbed," Dan said.

"Yeah, a disturbed dad. And her mom died on her, so she's got it bad enough. And Bud—"

Will felt his throat thickening. He had to stop and swallow hard before he could talk again.

"Bud's worried about Abe—who could maybe die—which is my fault to begin with—so even if I told him what I'm trying to do for him, he'd probably say, 'Don't do me any favors.' "

Dan nodded thoughtfully, his eyes following the rising smoke. "You've given this a lot of thought," he said. "And prayer, I'm sure."

"It's all I think *and* pray about!"

"And you've listened."

"I've tried. Quebi says Jesus wants me to know what to do and He'll show me. I haven't seen it yet."

"I think you're seeing it right now," Dan said.

"I am?"

"Here we are, just the two of us, in the Holy Silence. Those two motormouth girls are asleep—" his eyes twinkled at Will, "—and you can talk without getting your friend Miguel tangled up in it. You're always taking care of your friends, Will. That's why they're so devoted to you." He put up his hand. "I know you're going to say you didn't take care of Abe, but that's something different entirely. Let's concentrate on something you can really do something about. You interested?"

Will could only nod.

Dan nodded too, and closed his eyes. "Feel the Holy Silence of God, Will?" he said.

Will let his eyelids fall shut and waited. "It's quiet," he said.

"That's God's voice. Let's pray to Him."

And so they prayed, both of them, whispering Will's struggle to God in the Holy Silence, asking for His directions. It was a good and peaceful thing, and it made Will want to draw nearer to Dan and pray more.

It was the wee hours of the morning before they stopped. A fine drizzle was misting the air, and the two of them sat together under Dan's poncho, feeling the spray on their faces.

"I still don't know what to do," Will said.

"But do you feel different?"

"Do I *feel* different?" Will said. "I don't know what you mean."

"Are you exactly the same boy you were when we started to pray last night? When you were twisted up like a bag of knots?"

Will didn't have to consider that for long before he shook his head. "I don't feel like I have to do something right this minute."

Dan grinned back at him, a mustache of misty rain glowing on his upper lip. "That's one of the fruits of prayer. Patience. You may not know what to do this very minute, but you have the patience to wait for the answer."

"Wait'll I tell Mom I have patience now," Will said. "She'll probably kiss your feet!"

Dan stood up and stretched, and Will did the same. The dampness had put kinks in his legs that he wasn't sure he could ever iron out.

"You know something?" Dan said. "We didn't even have supper last night. Those three are going to come out of that tent ready to eat the firewood. I'd better get some breakfast going—"

He stopped abruptly, and spread his hands out at his sides. His face went tight with sudden attention.

"What is it?" Will said.

"Get down, Will!" Dan cried. "Get down!"

Will dropped to the ground and felt Dan come down on top of him. Beneath them, the ground began to shake.

✦ ✦ ✦

Chapter Fifteen

*T*he earth trembled for so long, Will was sure it was going to open up and swallow them.

The horses were tossing their heads, screaming out whinnies as they strained against the reins that tethered them to the trees. Will could hear cries from inside Dan's tent, and he raised his head to call out to Olive and Fawn and Miguel. Dan shoved his face back down to the dirt, but not before Will saw the sky—and gasped.

Everything above him was alive with the flash of a lightning bolt, and yet instead of flickering away, its unearthly glow stayed in the air.

Finally the upheaval stopped, though for several seconds the trees continued to rain pine cones, ripped too early from their branches. Even after that, Will could hear Olive and Fawn shouting from the tent.

"What happened?"

"Dad! Dad—are you all right?"

Dan rolled off of Will and got on all fours, but he didn't stand up.

"Stay in the tent," he called over his shoulder. "Don't come out 'til I tell you!"

"What happened, Dan?" Will said.

Dan searched the sky above the mountains and shook his head.

"I don't know," he said, "but look at that."

Will scrambled up to his knees and looked where Dan was pointing. The southwestern sky was one large cloud, suspended like a frozen fountain on its way up. Even as they watched, it began to fall; the same force that had pushed it upward now seemed to be pulling it down.

"What kind of storm is that?" Will said.

"That's no storm," Dan said. "That was an explosion."

"You mean like a bomb? Here?"

Dan shook his head and put an absent hand on Will's shoulder as he continued to study the cloud. "It wasn't like any bomb I've ever seen, and I've seen plenty. I don't like it. I don't like it at all."

"Dad?" Fawn called from the tent. "Can we come out now?"

Dan tore his eyes from the sky, which still seemed to be falling toward them, and nodded at the tent. "Come on out and get packed up, kids," he said. "We're heading home."

The sky was so eerie and the air so thick with dust and uncertainty, no one even complained as they took down the tents and put away the food they'd never gotten to eat.

"I'm sorry, kids," Dan said when they'd mounted the horses. "Something very strange is happening. I just think we'd be better off back in Santa Fe where maybe they know what's going on."

Even Will didn't protest, although he did give Los Alamos one last wistful look over his shoulder as they rode south.

One thing's for sure, he thought. *Whatever that explosion was, it didn't come from up there.*

What was it Eduardo Fernandez had said—weapons of mass destruction? If that was what they'd seen, it looked like Los Alamos— and the Manhattan Project—had nothing to do with it. The explosion had come from the opposite direction.

Maybe he is just "disturbed," Will thought. *But then, what are they doing up there that Bud thinks we should stay away from?*

The answer didn't come, but this time, Will knew to wait.

But that was hard to do when they reached the ranch that afternoon, tired and damp and hungry. Señora Otero was just putting a bowl of Spanish rice and chicken on the table when Mom arrived. One look at her face, and Will put down his fork.

"What's wrong, Mama Hutchie?" Fawn said. "Did the whole town blow up?"

"Fawn, honestly!" Olive said.

"Well, there was that big explosion thing. I betcha most of New Mexico blew up!"

Mom shook her head as she sank into a chair next to Fawn and rested a hand on her arm. "The afternoon paper says it was an accident in an ammunition dump."

"What's ammunition?"

"Bullets and stuff," Will said. He leaned toward his mother. "What's the matter, Mom? It's not just the explosion, is it?"

"No," Mom said. The fingers on Fawn's arm clutched it tighter. "It's Abe. He's taken a turn for the worse."

"Is he dying?" Fawn said.

"No, he's not dying!" Will said. "He's not, is he, Mom?"

"It doesn't look good. I've talked Bud into letting you kids go and say—well, go and see him."

"What about Tina?" Señora Otero said.

"They have her sedated," Mom said. "Between being exhausted and being hysterical, she wasn't doing anyone any good, least of all herself."

"Sedated means they gave her medicine to make her sleep," Olive whispered to Fawn.

Will got to his feet somehow and stumbled toward the door.

"Why don't I follow with the other kids in my car?" he heard Mr. T. say.

But Will didn't care how they got there. He just wanted to see Abe.

For once, the hospital corridor was empty and silent. Mom led Will into the room where Abe was lying in a bed with bottles and tubes hanging over it. Will's big pal looked helpless and frail in the midst of it all, and Will hung back just inside the door.

"It's all right, Son," Mom whispered to him. "He doesn't know any of this is happening to him. He's resting."

Will looked at her for one more nod of reassurance before he walked across the room to the bed. It seemed to take him a long, gray time to get there, and yet he was by Abe's side all too soon. Abe's face looked pasty, so that it was hard to tell his eyes and lips from the rest of his face. His chest moved up and down with a rattle. Other than that, he lay still as a stone.

Will wanted to cry out to the whole hospital—to every nurse and doctor and orderly who had touched him: *This is not Abe! This is not my pal! What have you done with him?*

But it was so deadly quiet, he didn't want to make a sound.

Is this a Holy Silence, God? Can You talk to me through this? Can You tell me what to do?

There was only the picture of Dad hanging on because that was all he could do. Will put his face close to Abe's.

"Abe?" Will whispered. "I know you're hurting, pal, but you've gotta hang on. You've gotta have endurance. I know you don't know what that means, but you can feel it. I need you, pal—I really do. I just want you to know how sorry I am that you got hurt."

Will could feel the tears streaming down his face, but he didn't stop to try to keep them from coming or even to smear them away.

"You're smart enough to make a choice, pal," Will said. "So I'm doing what Dan told me—I'm telling you what I know—and then you get to choose for yourself."

He glanced back over his shoulder. Mom had left the room. He and Abe were alone. Still, Will put his lips very close to Abe's ear.

"Bud—he's involved with the people at the Manhattan Project," he whispered. "I don't know what that is, and I'm not sure he does either. But it has something to do with Los Alamos and the secret stuff they're doing. At least, that's what Olive's dad says. I know he's not right in the head these days, but he said they're making weapons of mass destruction up there that could kill a lot of people, and I bet the Hibiscus Lady told him that. I don't think Bud knows about that, so I'm just trying to find out what I can so he can make a good choice." Will watched one of his tears splash onto Abe's face, but he pushed on. "I know now that I have to tell the people that are involved so they can choose. I shoulda told you and Olive. I probably shoulda told some grown-ups. I always mess up that way. But I'm learning to be different. So please don't die, Abe. I want you to see me being different. I wanna be a better friend to you. I need you, Abe! Please don't die!"

Will felt himself caving in. His head was bowing toward Abe's chest when he felt a hand on his shoulder. He looked up into Bud's eyes.

"He can't die," Will said. "Don't let him die, Bud."

Bud put his arms, warm and clammy with sweat, around Will and pulled him in. Through his own sobbing, Will could feel Bud crying too.

"I can't stop him from dying, Will," he said in a thick voice. "That's God's choice now."

"But it was my choice that caused it—"

"No, Will, no." Bud pushed Will just far enough away so that he could hold him by the shoulders and look in his eyes. "The fall Abe took wouldn't have hurt another person the way it did him. His body has other problems—things that would have turned on him sooner or later. He doesn't heal like other people. His heart is weak. His lungs are weak."

Will was shaking his head. He knew his face was a bewildered mess.

"It was easier for Tina to blame you than to blame God," Bud said. "But it isn't even God's fault. It's no one's fault. All I know is that God is taking care of him, whatever happens."

"He can't die," Will said.

"Yes, he can. Maybe we just have to let him go."

"No!" Will didn't care that his voice was probably going to bring every nurse in the place running. "We have to help him hang on!" he cried. "It's our only choice!"

He jerked away from Bud and twisted himself back to Abe. His friend's eyes were open, gazing at the ceiling like a pair of glass marbles.

"He's awake!" Will cried. "Bud—he's awake! He's hanging on!"

"What's happened, Bud? What is it?"

It was Tina, crashing through the door behind them, knocking them both aside as she hurled herself toward Abe. His eyes closed, and Tina threw her body across his chest. The day of the accident, Will had thought he would never see a human cry harder than Tina had that day. He'd been wrong.

"Son, you need to step outside," said a voice from a starched uniform beside him.

"He's awake—I want to talk to him!" Will cried.

"Come on—outside—that's a good boy—"

Will wrenched himself away from her, his hands flailing for Abe. But Tina and Bud were leaning over him, their backs like a wall that cut Will off from him. Slapping away the nurse's hands, Will lunged for the door. He had to find Mom.

But the only person in the hallway was Aunt Hildy Helen.

"Where's my mom?" Will said.

"I haven't seen her," Hildy said. "I'm looking for Olive—" She stopped and looked closely at Will. "Are you all right?"

"They say he's dying, but he's not! He just opened his eyes after I talked to him—I saw him!" Will could feel his voice winding up out of control, but he couldn't stop it, and he didn't try. "They're just gonna let him go—and they can't do that!"

He was out of breath. As he gasped for air, it suddenly occurred to him that he was telling all of this to Hildy Helen, the aunt who couldn't focus on a normal conversation, much less somebody's hysterical ranting.

"I gotta find my mom," he said.

He started off, his eyes barely seeing through the tears, but Aunt Hildy Helen caught him by the arm. When he tried to pull away, she got hold of the other one, too. She was stronger than she looked.

"Willie," she said. "I tell you what. I'll go in and see what I can find out about Abe."

"But—"

"You're a kid. They'll sweep you out like a dust bunny. I'll go in with Bud—you find Olive."

"I don't want Olive. I want my mom!"

"Listen to me."

It wasn't the fact that Aunt Hildy Helen was speaking with all the firmness of Mr. T. or Mom that made Will stop pulling away and focus his attention on her; it was the fact that she no longer had that vacant look in her eyes. She was probably more there than he was.

"Listen to me," she said again. "We have to find Olive. Her father is not in the sanitarium."

"Then he's out on a pass—"

"No pass. They've taken away his pass privileges."

Will stared at her. "You mean he escaped?"

"Slipped away when nobody was looking." Aunt Hildy let go of Will's arms. "We need to find out if she knows where he might have gone. Find her and bring her back here, and by then I'll have found out about Abe."

Will looked longingly at the door to Abe's room. He could still taste the salt of his tears, and he knew his nose was dripping down his chin.

"Go, Willie," Aunt Hildy Helen whispered. "And here—" She stuck a tissue into his hand and gave him a nudge.

Although it was hard to move away from Abe's room, it only took Will two steps to realize that it was better to have something to do than to stand there and wait.

The problem now was where to find Olive. He'd heard Mr. T. say he was going to bring everybody else in his car. If so, they should be here by now.

Will charged down the hall to the waiting room, but the metal chairs were empty. Then he careened around the corner to the front door to check the parking lot for Mr. T.'s car. He plowed straight into Miguel, who had Mr. T. and Señora Otero behind him.

"Where's Olive?" Will said.

"Are you all right, Son?" Mr. T. said. He squinted down at Will. "Is Abe—?"

"He's not gonna die!" Will cried. "But I have to find Olive—where is she?"

"She was feeling a little shaky about all this," Señora Otero said. "She said she wanted to see her father first."

"No!" Will said. "He's not there—he escaped! I have to tell her!"

There was a stunned pause. Señora Otero and Mr. T. looked at each other, and they seemed to be having a conversation with their eyes.

"Go," Señora Otero finally said to Will.

Mr. T. nodded. "Better she should hear it from you than some orderly . . ."

Will didn't hear the rest of what he said. He turned on his heel and ran for the elevator.

When he got there, he could hear it creaking somewhere in the building, and he abandoned it for the stairs. With every step he raged at himself.

I should've told her about her dad before. I should've told her he was going nuts about the Manhattan Project.

I should've let her make her own choice.

Now the only thing to do was pray, and Will did as his boots slipped and slid out the hall door and down the hallway toward the sanitarium nurses' station. By the time he skidded to a stop, there was a crisp white uniform blocking his way.

"Slow down," she said. "This is a hospital, not a playground—"

"Olive Fernandez!" Will said. "I have to find Olive Fernandez— her dad's Eduardo—"

"She just got on the elevator, headed down," the nurse said. "And I suggest you do the same—"

Will left her in the wake of his scuff marks as he fled for the stairs again. He was halfway down the steps before the hall door closed behind him.

Please—just let her be there, he prayed.

Will threw open the doors into the main hallway, already pointing his way toward the elevator. But its doors were just sighing shut, and the operator was saying to his passengers, "Going up." Olive was nowhere in sight.

"Olive!" Will shouted.

Heart in his throat, Will sailed toward the corner, headed for Abe's room. More than likely Olive had gone to find Señora Otero or Mr. T. And Aunt Hildy Helen would know about Abe by now.

But just as he got to the corner, he heard a man's voice behind him say, "Whoa there, girlie! You might want to watch where you're going, hon—"

Will looked over his shoulder, nearly slamming into the wall. The man was an orderly. He was talking to Olive, who dodged the cart he was pushing and didn't look back as she disappeared down the front steps.

"Olive!" Will shouted. He hurled himself after her, nearly colliding with the same cart.

"What is this, a speedway today?" the man said.

Will didn't bother to answer.

✝ ✝ ✝

*T*here was no one on the front steps when Will flew out the hospital door, and as he looked wildly up and down the street, he found it empty as well. There was nothing but the sunset burning above the adobe buildings.

"Olive?" Will cried out. "Where are you?"

There was no answer—at least not from Olive. But there was a voice in his head, a thought that seemed to know what to do.

I can't make the same mistake with Olive. I have to tell her about her dad.

Will took the first three steps down in one leap. And then he stopped.

I didn't tell anybody what I was doing before. That's how I got Abe hurt.

I can't do that again.

He turned to head for the front door when movement across the street caught his eye. It was Olive, emerging from the shadows and stretching her neck to look down the street.

"Olive!" Will called out.

If she heard him, she didn't show it. She merely turned to peer through the gathering darkness up the road.

Please, God, Will prayed. *Just don't let her be gone when I get back.*

He shoved his way through the front door, and once more nearly plowed into the orderly with his cart.

"Sir?" he said. "Could you do me a favor?"

"You could do *me* one! You and your friends could stop trying to run me down!"

"No—please—go to Abraham Kates's room and tell whoever's there that I—that Will—went out to get Olive."

"Tell Abraham Lincoln that Bill went out to get olives," the orderly said. He narrowed his eyes at Will. "Are you tryin' to give me the business, kid?"

"No, please! *Abe Kates's* room. Will went to find Olive—she's a girl!" Will could feel his voice threatening to crack. "Please—it's important!"

"You all right, kid?" the man said.

"No! That's why you gotta tell 'em!"

Will didn't wait to see if the man nodded or shook his head. There was no more time to waste. He had to find Olive—before another one of his choices went bad.

Olive had disappeared by the time Will got back outside. Forcing himself not to panic, he headed north, in the direction he'd last seen her looking. If she'd turned the corner and gone up San Francisco Street, she could be swallowed up in the Saturday evening crowd at LaFonda, but he had to try.

His heart was hammering like a woodpecker's beak by the time he reached the outside patio at the hotel, and there was still no sign of Olive. The only familiar face he saw was one with a pipe in his mouth, blowing smoke from under the snap-brim of a straw hat. If anyone would have noticed a frantic girl, it would be an FBI agent. Will ran to him, dodging the mariachis as he went.

"Agent Graves—sir?" he said, even before he reached him in his usual rustic leather chair.

The man looked up at Will and removed the pipe from his mouth. "Can I help you?" he said.

He had a matter-of-fact voice, like the men on radio news. It was somehow comforting to Will.

"Did you see a girl running by here?" Will said. "About as tall as me. She's Hispanic— dark hair, kinda bushy."

"That sounds like half the young girls in the city," the agent said dryly.

"No—she's different!" Will said, craning his neck to get a good look at the doorway. "She was probably crying. Did you see anybody like that?"

"Who is this girl? Is she in trouble?"

"Her name's Olive Fernandez," Will said. "She's trying to find her father—he was in the sanitarium, only he escaped—and *he* could be in trouble—"

And then Will stopped, mid-sentence. Olive was coming out the LaFonda front door. She was talking to a blonde woman.

The woman with the ever-present red flower tucked behind her ear.

"Never mind," Will said to Agent Graves. "I found her."

As Will wove his way amid the people making their lazy way into the hotel, Olive gave the woman a final nod. The moment Olive turned her head, she saw Will. Her eyes, as puffy as Will knew his were, lit up, and she hurried toward him.

"I tried to get to you to tell you your dad was gone—" Will said.

But Olive shook her head and, grabbing him by the sleeve, pulled him through the patio toward the street. As they went, she looked over her shoulder and waved to Hibiscus Lady.

"Does she know where your dad is?" Will said.

"She says she does. She says he's gone to the movies." Olive sniffed. "My father hates the movies."

"So where are we going?"

"We're going to pretend we're headed for the theater, and then when she leaves the hotel we're going to follow her and she's going to lead us to him."

She pulled Will into the indented entrance to Woolworth's, which had already closed for the day.

"You think she doesn't want you to find him?" Will said. "But why not? I thought she was his friend. She went to visit him at the sanitarium."

"Because she's part of that thing up at Los Alamos."

Will nodded. "Yeah, it makes sense."

"No, it doesn't. It makes no sense at all! What could my father possibly have to do with whatever they're doing at Los Alamos?"

"He hates it, that's what."

Olive shifted her eyes back to the glass, searching LaFonda with her gaze. "I know you don't like my father, Will, but that's not fair."

"No—I heard him yelling at Reverend Bud after the wedding, after you'd all left for the reception. He was saying Bud shouldn't be praying with people who were making weapons of mass destruction that could kill thousands of innocent people. Bud said that was just a rumor."

"There she goes!" Olive said suddenly. "I have to follow her. I have to find my dad."

"Then I'm going with you," Will said. "Come on—before she loses us!"

It was hard to keep Hibiscus Lady in their sights, between the Saturday folks coming into town and the darkness that was quickly falling as the sun sank behind the mountains. At St. Francis Cathedral, where San Francisco Street ended, Will couldn't see her anywhere, but Olive pointed up Alameda. Hibiscus Lady's back was fading amid the adobe walls.

"We're far enough back so we can run," Will said.

He grabbed Olive's wrist and pulled her into the trees that lined the dirt walkway. Together they ran, crouching low to stay in the shadows. Gradually they were able to gain on Hibiscus, who seemed completely unconcerned that anyone might be following her.

Will's heart started to lift. Maybe they would get to Olive's father in time to get him back to St. Vincent's—before there was any trouble for Olive.

I have to do this, Will told himself. *I let Abe down. I can't do it to Olive.*

But as they came to Paseo de Peralta, Will's steps slowed and he put out his hand in front of Olive like the sign at a railroad crossing.

Hibiscus Lady crossed the street to the Castillo Bridge—and went under it. The memory of Agent Graves emerging from that very spot flashed in Will's mind like a flicker of lightning.

"What are you doing, Will?" Olive whispered. "We have to follow her!"

"No," Will whispered back. "I think we should go back and get help. We need a grown-up."

"Then *you* go back," Olive said. She shoved his hand out of the way. "I'm going down there for my dad."

Before Will could stop her, Olive ran across the street, where Hibiscus Lady had disappeared under the bridge.

"Olive!" he hissed.

But he already knew she wasn't going to stop. His heart pounding again, Will followed her.

When he got to the bridge, she was crouched against the railing, her ear plastered to it.

"This is dangerous," Will whispered. "Agent Graves comes here—"

Olive put her finger to her lips. *Listen,* she mouthed to him.

Below, voices were being raised to a volume louder than mere conversation, as though the two people had forgotten they were trying to conceal themselves. One voice belonged to a woman. The other was clearly that of Eduardo Fernandez.

"I have been waiting for two days for you to show," the woman said in a deep voice that reminded Will of cigarettes. Will could only assume it was Hibiscus Lady. She certainly *sounded* like a person who would wear a big red flower behind her ear. "If you hadn't shown up today, I was going to find someone else—"

"I'm here. I'm ready. Give me the last of it."

There was a long silence. Olive put her lips near Will's ear. "The last of what?" she whispered.

Will shrugged. He wasn't sure he wanted to know. He *was* sure he wanted Mr. T. or Dan here.

Hibiscus Lady spoke again. "My husband says the test this morning was a success. That means we don't have much time to get the last of the formula to our contact." There was a pause. "I have it here for you to pass on to him—the final piece of the formula."

"Our *contact?*" Eduardo said. His voice was tight, and Will cringed. From the sound of it, it wouldn't be long before Eduardo would be raging like a crazed goose. "You never called him a 'contact' before. You said he was another objector—like myself—locked up in the sanitarium because we do not believe in mass destruction!"

"What does it matter what I call him?"

"What matters is what he's going to do with it," Eduardo said. "You told me he knew people—people who would destroy the formula when we got it all for him, so they could go no further with the bomb!"

"Don't be absurd," Hibiscus Lady said. She gave a deep laugh. "You don't think they have copies up there? That those eggheads don't have it all memorized?" Will heard paper rustling as if she were passing something to him. "It's worth a great deal of money—and I'm selling it. Now are you going to deliver it or not?"

Will glanced at Olive. She was squeezing the railing so hard, her arms were shaking.

Please, Eduardo, Will wanted to shout at him. *Please say no!*

"No," Eduardo said. "I want the destruction stopped. That was the plan I agreed to: that I would take the formula for the bomb to him because he could not leave St. Vincent's as I could—and that *his* wife would see that it was destroyed. It would be a trail no one could follow." Will could hear Eduardo's voice shaking. "I did not agree to his selling it. I thought he was just like me—"

Will heard the crunch of footsteps, and he yanked at Olive's jacket. "Get down!" he whispered.

Together they flattened themselves even lower to the ground, and Will watched the end of the bridge where he was sure any minute Eduardo Fernandez would appear.

But below, a loud click broke the silence, followed by Hibiscus Lady's low voice.

"Hold it right there, Eduardo," she said. "Don't take another step or I'll shoot."

‡ •‡• ‡

Chapter Seventeen

*B*efore Will could stop her, Olive sprang up and leaped over him to get to the end of the bridge. To his horror, she screamed— "Daddy!"

Olive kicked up an avalanche of sand and gravel as she scrambled down the riverbank and disappeared under the bridge. Will tore after her, a vision of her hurling herself at her father clear in his head.

But when Will rounded the end of the bridge railing, it wasn't her father's arms he saw Olive in. It was Hibiscus Lady who was holding her—with Olive's back to her, her arm around Olive's neck. The gun they had heard was pointed at Olive's head.

They both faced Eduardo Fernandez, who seemed frozen in mid-run below them, all but his eyes, which darted from Olive's face to that of her captor. He didn't appear to see Will, nor did Hibiscus Lady. It gave Will a chance to creep back to the bridge and hide behind the railing. Half of his mind was already going wild, shouting at him to run for help. But the other half wouldn't let him leave Olive, and that was the half that kept him clinging to the bridge railing and watching.

"Give it back to me, Eduardo," Hibiscus Lady said, "or so help me, I'll pull the trigger."

For the first time, Will saw that Olive's father did have the paper in his hands as he'd thought he'd heard. *That must be the formula she just handed him,* Will thought. *The formula for the bomb.*

But what bomb? Surely Eduardo couldn't be right about "weapons of mass destruction."

"I'll do it," Hibiscus Lady said. "I'll shoot her."

As if to assure him, she tightened her grip on Olive. From where he crouched, watching in terror, Will could see Olive's eyes bulging. But she didn't make a sound, and she didn't move. She only watched her father as he made his choice.

"You won't hurt an innocent girl," Eduardo said.

Hibiscus Lady laughed. "I'm about to sell a secret that will probably kill thousands of them. Do I look like I care? I'm going to be busy using that money to make up for the last two miserable years of living on the Hill in a metal shack with a bunch of crackpot scientists."

She adjusted the gun in her hand. Will's heart was beating so hard, he could feel it throbbing in his throat.

Give her back the stupid paper, Eduardo! Will wanted to scream at him. *We'll get it away from her later—just don't let her shoot Olive!*

"All right," Eduardo said. His voice shook and so did his hand as he held out the rolled paper.

"Put it on the ground and back away," Hibiscus Lady said.

Eduardo nodded and set the paper carefully on the riverbed. Will's thoughts began to talk to him.

As soon as she lets go, I'll grab Olive and we'll run. Eduardo can get the gun and take the paper back from the woman. I can do this. Please, God, help me do this—

But Hibiscus Lady didn't take her hands off of Olive. She inched toward the paper with Olive in front of her like a shield, the gun still pressed to her temple.

Will's thoughts went wild again, but he pulled them all together into one.

Rising slowly, he crept from the bridge and made his way down.

Just as Hibiscus Lady leaned over to pick up the paper, bending Olive down with her, Will yelled, "Hey, lady!"

She jumped like a startled rabbit and whirled around, the hibiscus blossom flying from behind her ear. The arm holding the gun flailed crazily for a moment before she found Will. The other arm loosened its hold on Olive, and even as Will watched the woman take aim at him, he saw Olive wriggle free and grab Hibiscus Lady's wrist.

The woman's eyes flashed, and she grabbed Olive's hair with her free hand and pulled. Olive yowled, but not as loudly as Eduardo. He leaped on the woman from behind, knocking both Olive and her to the ground. The gun jarred free and landed with a dull thud at Will's feet. Hibiscus Lady, Olive, and Eduardo fell in a tangled heap.

Will leaned over to pick up the gun, his mind reeling.

"Don't touch it, Son," said a matter-of-fact voice behind him. "Just leave it there and back away."

Will didn't argue. He only looked up, frozen, to see Agent Graves and another man in a snap-brim hat brush past him toward the wrestling match that was going on in the riverbed, and then backed away from the gun, straight into the arms of still another straw-hatted man.

"There's a piece of paper on the ground there," Will said. "I think you're gonna want to pick that up."

"We've got it handled, kid," the agent said.

Below him, Will heard Olive calling his name. He looked down in time to see her hurtling toward him, face crumpling like a wad of newspaper. He didn't have time to dodge before she threw her arms around his neck and held on. But she was crying so hard, he didn't peel her away. He just said, "I think it's gonna be okay now, Olive. I really think it's gonna be okay."

There was some doubt about that for the next few hours, however.

Hibiscus Lady was taken into custody by enough men in gray suits and snap-brim hats to fill up the Plaza Café, or so it seemed to Will. But so was Eduardo Fernandez, and that sent Olive into a rage. It took Will and two other men to hold her back as an agent pushed

Eduardo's head down and deposited him in the backseat of a car that was built like the Sherman tanks Will had seen in *LIFE* magazine. If Mr. T. and Señora Otero hadn't arrived just then to take over with Olive, Will was sure she would have broken free and chased the car down the Paseo de Peralta.

"He's not a criminal!" she shouted at Mr. T. "They're treating him like a criminal, and he's not!"

"I know, darlin'," Mr. T. said. Señora Otero folded her long arms around Olive and stroked her hair.

Will reflected later that the three of them looked just like a family right them. But at that moment, he was focused on Mom, who arrived looking as if she herself were in custody. She had two more gray-suited men with her, one on each side. By now, the riverbank was swarming with them. He had never been so glad to see his mother, and he didn't care that she hugged him hard in front of all of them.

"Don't be mad, Mom," he said. "I couldn't just let Olive go looking for her father by herself. That lady held a gun to her head—she could've been shot! Just don't be mad. I tried to let you know—I asked that orderly person to tell you—"

Mom pressed her hand to the side of Will's face. "Son," she said, "I think that's the least of your worries right now."

She looked over his head and nodded. Agent Graves curled his fingers firmly around Will's arm.

"If you'll just come with me, Son," he said.

Will looked wildly at his mother, but she didn't pounce on the agent. She just nodded.

"They just want to talk to you," she said. "Tell them the truth and you'll be fine."

Agent Graves gave Will's arm a little tug.

"Aren't you coming?" Will said to Mom.

"No—they need to talk to you alone. I'll be right outside the car. Don't worry."

But Will was beyond worrying. His heart pounded like a sledge-hammer as Agent Graves led him to one of a line of long black cars parked on Castillo Bridge, and it pounded harder when he saw another agent escorting Olive to the next vehicle in line.

"She didn't do anything wrong," Will said to Agent Graves. "She was just trying to protect her father. He's not okay in the head—"

"We know all that," Agent Graves said, never changing the radio-news tone of his voice. "We just want to ask you both a few questions. After you."

He opened the car door and motioned for Will to get in. Will slid across the backseat, Agent Graves sliding in beside him and closing the door. For a frantic moment, Will looked for the door handle on his side, but there was none. Between them and the front seat was a sheet of what looked like glass. On the other side of it, a man sat in the driver's seat, staring straight ahead. Will tried to swallow, but his heart in his throat wouldn't let him.

"Look, I wasn't trying to steal secrets or anything," he said. "I just—"

"Relax, Will," Agent Graves said. "All I want you to do is tell me everything you know about what happened tonight. Tell me the truth, and you'll be back home with your mom before you know it."

He was still using his nothing-but-the-facts voice, but there was a kindness in the agent's eyes that made Will think he must have kids of his own. Although Will's heart was working its way right up into his mouth, he tried to settle back against the seat.

"Tell me anything that you think has to do with what you saw tonight," Agent Graves said.

Will started at the beginning and told it all: seeing the woman in her Jeep at the locked gate with the machine gun emplacements, being chased off by the soldier with the gun, being warned by Reverend Bud about staying away from Los Alamos, seeing Agent Graves himself at the prayer meeting where the Manhattan Project was mentioned, hearing Eduardo Fernandez raging at the pastor, and seeing the Hibiscus Lady visiting Eduardo at the sanitarium. He wound up with tonight's events—and a plea.

"Please don't do anything to Reverend Bud," he said. "His son's probably gonna die—because of me—because of all this. He's got enough trouble."

"Don't worry about the Reverend," Agent Graves said. He patted his pocket, as if he were looking for his pipe, and settled for a toothpick which he parked between his teeth as he leaned toward Will.

"You saved your friend's life tonight," he said.

"She'd have done the same for me—"

Agent Graves put up his hand. His eyes were stern now. "My turn to do the talking," he said. "Your turn to listen. Understood?"

Will clamped his lips together and nodded.

"You're going to want to tell your friends how you saved the Fernandez girl's life and helped the FBI save an important document."

Will raised his hand.

"Yeah?" Agent Graves said.

"A document—that's the roll of paper they were fighting over?"

"Right. It's going to be a big temptation to tell everybody about it. Let's face it, you were a hero." Agent Graves slowly shook his head, his eyes never leaving Will's face. "But you can't tell a soul—not one single person. You can't tell your mother what you know, or your best friend, or your pastor friend. You can't even discuss it with the Fernandez girl. You both have to pretend this never happened."

Will raised his hand again. Agent Graves nodded.

"Why?" Will said.

"Because it's bigger than both of us, Son. Important people who know what they're doing have made some secret decisions, and those decisions stand. If you mess that up—if you let any of this out—it could affect the outcome of the war. Do you understand?"

"No," Will said.

Agent Graves leaned even closer, so that his nose nearly touched Will's despite the snap-brim hat. He was so close, Will could see the tobacco stains on his teeth as he readjusted the toothpick.

"Do you want your daddy to come home?" he said.

"Well, yeah. Of course I do—"

"You talking about this to anybody could make the difference between him coming home and you never seeing him again. It's that important, Son."

Will could feel the blood draining from his face. He kept his eyes locked to the agent's as he shook his head.

"Then I'll never say a word," he said. "Never."

Agent Graves reached up and squeezed Will's shoulder. "Good choice," he said. "You're a good man." Then he pulled back and put out his hand. Will shook it.

"Thank you for what you did tonight," he said. "But from now on, if you see anything suspicious, you come to me."

"Yes, sir," Will said.

His voice shook, and he could feel the beads of sweat on his upper lip. His heart resettled itself into its normal place as Agent Graves tapped on the glass between them and the front seat, and the man in the driver's seat got out and opened Will's door. It was all he could do not to leap from it and run all the way to Canyon Road—where he intended to remain until he stopped shaking.

But Agent Graves stopped him with a hand on his shoulder. "Hey," he said, taking the toothpick out of his mouth.

"Yes, sir?" Will said.

"Your dad's going to be mighty proud of you when he gets home."

"But I can't tell him about this," Will said.

"No," Agent Graves said. "But you won't have to. He's going to be proud of who you are." Then he replaced the pick between his teeth and slid out of the car.

Will started to climb out his side, but Mom was there, and she motioned for him to scoot over.

"Where are we going?" he said as she got in beside him and an agent closed the door.

"To the hospital," she said. "Somebody wants to see you."

Will's heart began its ascent to his throat again, but he didn't ask questions. He sank back into the seat and let Mom hold his hand. She didn't ask any questions either, except one.

"Are you all right, Son?" she said.

"I don't know," Will said.

She nodded. "I think that's the right answer."

Aunt Hildy Helen was waiting for them when the agent let them out of the car in front of the hospital.

"Still the same?" Mom said to her.

Aunt Hildy nodded.

"He went back unconscious?" Will said. Until now he'd had to push Abe out of his mind, but he was back now, and it was as painful as ever.

Mom and Aunt Hildy Helen were exchanging glances around him.

"What?" Will said. "He didn't die while I was gone?"

"No!" Mom said. "Come on, you'll see."

Mom took him by the arm on one side and, to his surprise, Aunt Hildy did the same on the other. His feet barely seemed to touch the floor as they half-carried him into the hospital, around the corner, and down the hall to Abe's room. Dan, Conchita, Fawn, and Miguel were standing against the wall outside. The instant Fawn spotted Will, she bounded toward him.

"Where have you been?" she said. "He keeps asking where you are!"

"Bud?" Will said. It was something he hadn't thought of—he wouldn't even be able to warn Bud that the FBI was going to stuff him in the backseat of a car and ask him questions—

"No, not Bud, silly!" Fawn said.

But Conchita stopped her with a click of her tongue.

"What's going on?" Will said.

Mom gave him a nudge toward Abe's door. "You'll see," she said.

"Is Tina in there?" Will said.

It was Aunt Hildy Helen who nudged him this time, harder than Mom. "You sure ask a lot of questions," she said. "You're worse than your father. Go *in* already!"

So Will did. Tina was indeed there, and Bud—but they were smiling. And Abe was smiling back at them, eyes wide open. When he saw Will, he let out a gurgle.

"Will!" he said. "Abey—better!"

Will could only stare. Only when Bud said, "It's okay—you can talk to him," did Will go slowly to the bed. Abe was still a mass of tubes and bottles and needles, but none of it seemed to be bothering him. The smile he gave Will was pasty, but it was a smile.

"So—are you okay, pal?" Will said.

"Abey okay!"

"Well, he's not 'okay,' " Tina said. "But he's going to be. If no one gets him too excited."

Will looked up in time to see Bud pat Tina's hand and shake his head ever so slightly at her. She was quiet.

"Whew, pal," Will said to Abe. He could feel tears making their way into his voice. "You had me scared. I never meant this to happen to you."

"Dad good," Abe said.

"You bet he's good." Will nodded, five times more than he needed to, he was sure. "He's the best man in the world, next to *my* dad, of course."

"Will good," Abe said.

Will hesitated on that one. It was Bud who answered.

"Will is *very* good," Bud said. "He's one of those 'best men' too."

Tina didn't join in, but she didn't jump at him across the bed like a guard dog, either.

The door opened then, and a starched nurse sailed in with a tray of more bottles and needles.

"It's time for our boy's medication," she said. "You know the rules—everybody out."

"I thought he was okay now," Will whispered to Bud as they filed out of the room.

"He's not going to be completely fine for a long time," Bud said. He ran his hand across his eyes, which were so puffy from weariness Will could hardly see them. "But, Will, that's not because of the injuries. While he's been here, they've discovered some things that have been ailing Abe all his life. He's going to make it, but it's going to take time—"

"And patience," Will said. "Then he *is* gonna be okay, because we've got that."

What Will could see of Bud's eyes filled up again. All he could do was nod at Will, and that was enough.

The next few weeks did require patience, the fruit of listening to God's voice in the silence that Dan had taught Will about. Some of the things that happened required choices. Some didn't. But Will felt himself knowing the difference more and more.

The Hutchinsons—Mom and Will and Aunt Hildy Helen—kept the radio on almost all the time as events seemed to be speeding up with the war. The Allies issued their final ultimatum to Japan for unconditional surrender, according to the agreement President Truman and the leaders of Great Britain and the Soviet Union had made at Potsdam. Japan didn't surrender, and on July 28, six Japanese cities were bombed. On August 1, four more had bombs dropped on them. Will wondered if the Allies had used the bombs they were making at Los Alamos, but he didn't say a word.

He tried to concentrate on the things he *could* change. Eduardo Fernandez was taken out of the St. Vincent's sanitarium and placed in Bruns Military Hospital. He had never served in the military himself, but it seemed the FBI wanted to keep a close eye on him while he was being treated for his "mental disturbance."

"Is Olive's dad ever going to be right in the head?" Will asked at dinner one night. "Is there something we oughta be doing about it? Olive cries half the time because she thinks he's gonna be like that forever."

To his surprise, it was Aunt Hildy Helen who answered. She was surprising him so much lately, he knew it was going to become normal pretty soon.

"Bruns is the best place for him," Aunt Hildy Helen said. "They're experts at treating what he's going through."

"What's he going through?" Will said.

"It's hard to explain. It's kind of the opposite of what happened to me. I saw so much suffering and destruction I couldn't take it anymore, so I shut it out. The problem is, when you shut one thing down, it all shuts down and I couldn't do anything, couldn't even feel anything."

"So, you weren't really crazy," Will said.

"William!" Mom said.

But Aunt Hildy Helen laughed, a husky chuckle that reminded him of Dad. "Oh, I'm definitely crazy," she said. "I'm just not shell-shocked anymore."

"So . . . what about Eduardo?" Will said.

"He sees the suffering and destruction in his head, without being there, because he's a passionate person. But unlike me, he feels *too* much and he can't get control of it. He was so frustrated about not being able to do anything about the war, he went a little out of his head."

"So you think he'll be okay?"

"That depends on him," Aunt Hildy Helen said. "I'm trying to help him and Olive."

Will looked down at his plate. Tears he hadn't expected blurred his view of the pile of kale.

"Will, what is it?" Mom said.

"Everybody's family is coming together: Dan and Conchita and Fawn, Abe and Bud and Tina, Olive and her dad—even Señora Otero and Mr. T. and Miguel seem like a family now."

Mom cleared her throat. "More than you know. Señora Otero and Mr. T. have told me they're going to be married, just as soon as they think Miguel is ready. He's still grieving for his father, and Mr. T. doesn't want them to get off on the wrong foot."

"And I'm happy for them, I really am," Will said. He blinked back the tears. "But what about us? I know there's you and me—and Aunt Hildy and Uncle Al—but—"

"But what about your father, right?" Will could feel Aunt Hildy's hand covering his on the tabletop. "You mean, it will never feel like a family without him."

Will nodded.

"Then I think you need to be helping me with the family tree," she said.

"Huh?"

"The tree I'm doing in the attic. It's for your dad when he comes home."

"Look, no offense," Will said, "but I don't think—"

"It's your choice," Aunt Hildy Helen said, "but it's one of the things that has given me hope since I've been here—besides your mom and you."

"Me?" Will said. "I haven't done anything except try to stay away from you because I thought you were nuts."

"William!" Mom said. "Enough with this 'crazy' theme!"

But Aunt Hildy was laughing, and it was more than a chuckle this time. Her eyes danced, and for the first time Will noticed that even though she didn't look like Dad with her dark hair and her big eyes, she *was* like him. She seemed to want to put her arms out and invite life in, just the way his father did.

"You've done more than you know," she said, "just by carrying on the Hutchinson strength and wit and—and just plain gutsiness. You've made me remember what it's like to be a Hutchinson kid." Aunt Hildy grinned at him. "And you do it so well."

"Does that mean getting in trouble and dragging everybody else with you?" Will said.

"That's it," Aunt Hildy said. "So what do you say we team up in the attic and make some real mischief with this tree? Let me give you back some of what you've given me."

"Why am I nervous about this all of a sudden?" Mom said. Her lips weren't just twitching. She was grinning bigger than Abe ever did.

Over the next few days, Will chose to spend his mornings riding the horses on Mr. T.'s ranch with Olive and Fawn and Miguel and Dan, his afternoons playing board games and reading books to Abe at the hospital, and his evenings in the dining room working with Aunt Hildy Helen on the family tree. Mom said it was too hot up in the attic and surrendered the dining room table to them to work at while she read through all the old family diaries and letters Aunt Hildy had collected.

The night of August 6, just as they were closing up for the night, a special news bulletin crackled its way onto the air. Aunt Hildy and Mom and Will crowded around the radio as though they could see the announcer. His news rooted them to the spot.

"The Allies have dropped a new kind of bomb on the Japanese city of Hiroshima," he said. "This is an atomic bomb, developed in Los Alamos, New Mexico. This is a bomb whose destructive capabilities can only be guessed at."

✢ ✤ ✢

Chapter Eighteen

*T*he next day, the newspaper headlines were two inches high with news of the atomic bombing. Three days later, there were more. On August 9, another such bomb had been dropped, this time on Nagasaki, Japan.

"This bomb is more devastating than anything previously used," the newspaper article said. "Even by the Germans in Europe."

At the Plaza Café, in Woolworth's, and even just passing through the Plaza, all Will and the kids heard was talk of the bomb.

"Did they have to kill innocent women and children?" some people said.

"But who knows how many more Americans will be killed if we don't stop this war now?" others said. "Maybe this is the only way to do it."

That, it seemed, was what President Truman had in mind. Once more the Hutchinsons—and the McHorses and Margretta Dietrich and the group from Mr. T.'s ranch—gathered around the radio in the Hutchinsons' living room to listen to his press conference. The president told the nation that the atomic bomb had been developed by the world's top scientists, working in various places around the country, to be used as a last resort to bring Japan to its knees.

"There will be a rain of ruin on Japan," he said, "if she fails to surrender unconditionally."

Mr. T. gave a long, low whistle.

"What are you thinking?" Mom said.

Mr. T. shook his head. "I had a lot of long talks with Yoji Lin when he and his family were living here. For a Japanese soldier, giving up to the enemy means losing face entirely. The Japanese would rather die than surrender."

"Then I guess there will be a rain of ruin on them," Dan said.

Everyone fell silent. Will met Olive's eyes across the room. They knew what it was all about now.

It must have been a hard choice for those people up there to build that bomb, Will thought. *No wonder Bud prayed with them.*

Bud didn't stop praying, either. A few days later, he announced that there would be a prayer vigil at the church. He said candles would be kept lit in the sanctuary and prayers said around the clock until Japan surrendered.

Will was prepared to beg Mom to let him go, but she was way ahead of him. She asked him what time slots he wanted before he even had a chance to start whining.

"Can't I just stay the whole night?" he said.

Her mouth twitched. "I was hoping you'd say that," she said.

So right after supper they went to the church, he and Mom and Aunt Hildy Helen. It was her first time at church since she had arrived in Santa Fe, except for the wedding, and she fell at once to her knees and stayed there for a very long time.

Dan and Conchita and Fawn arrived some time later, and Fawn sat next to Will, swinging her legs and watching the candle flames. If Will had bet she couldn't stay quiet for that long, he would have lost everything he had. She did whisper to him once, to say, "I'm praying that you get to have your dad home too. But if you don't, you can share mine."

Will wouldn't have minded having Dan for a dad—if he hadn't had an ache in his chest for his own father. The longer he prayed, the more it hurt. But it was a hurt he chose to hold onto, because to let go meant letting go of Dad, too. He'd learned that from Aunt Hildy.

Olive came to the church with Mr. T. and Señora Otero and Miguel. As she slipped into the pew on the other side of Will, she looked happier than she had since the night the FBI had taken her father away.

"What are you up to?" Will whispered to her.

"Mr. T. and Señora Otero are going to get married," she whispered back. "And they said if my dad agrees, they'll be my legal guardians. Miguel's going to be my brother."

Will waited for the pang of jealousy to hit him, but it didn't. How could it, he thought, with everyone around them praying that families would soon be pieced back together?

"He's not gonna make me wear a tie, is he?" Will whispered to Olive.

Olive grinned.

"Hey, Olive," he said, still under his breath.

"Yeah."

"I'm praying for those people up at Los Alamos. Are you?"

"Yeah. Is that what we saw that day when we were camping—the testing of the bomb?"

Will nodded.

"Then I'm praying for the people in Japan, too," she said.

Will bowed his head and did the same.

At about 2:00 A.M., Will could feel his eyelids getting heavy. Fawn and Olive were both stretched out on pews, asleep, and Miguel dozed with his head resting against Mr. T.'s shoulder. Will looked around for Mom, but she was on her knees with Aunt Hildy and Conchita and Señora Otero, their hands all clasped together in a ring of hope.

Will sighed. It was a lonely moment—until he felt a hand on his shoulder.

"How goes it?" Bud whispered to him.

"Okay, I guess," Will said. "I'm all prayed out. Is that bad?"

"You're still praying. Hopeful waiting is a prayer in itself."

He sat down on the pew next to Will and was quiet. But there was something Will needed to say.

"You've been kind of like a dad to me."

"And you're like a son to me, so that works out."

"Mr. T. and sometimes Quebi and now Dan have been, too," Will said, "but mostly you."

"It's been my pleasure."

Bud still watched the candles, a peacefulness about his pudgy face. But Will couldn't rest yet.

"Have you and Tina forgiven me for Abe getting hurt?"

"Of course we have. Tina's a little overprotective—but she'll come around. She knows Abe lights up when you come into the room, and that makes her happy."

"Then—you would still be like a dad to me, if my own dad doesn't—"

Will couldn't finish the sentence. He didn't have to. Bud looked at him with eyes shiny with candlelight and love.

"I would be honored," he said. "But don't let go yet, Will."

"Oh, I won't," Will said. "A Hutchinson always hangs on."

Not long after that, Will's eyes slammed shut. He woke up at dawn when Bud stood up, jouncing Will from his shoulder. Someone was standing in the doorway to the church, silhouetted in morning sunlight, yelling his head off.

"It's over!" he shouted. "The Japanese have surrendered! It's over!"

Sleepy heads popped up from their prayers all over the church, and the already wide-awake shouted and jumped over pews to get to one another. Amid the hugging—during which Will even let Olive and Fawn hug him—Mom found him. She pulled Will into her arms.

"It's over, Son," she said. "Thank God it's over." She pushed him out to look at him at arm's length. "He'll come home now," she said. "I know it."

Preparations were immediately made in Santa Fe for a celebration in the Plaza. The Hutchinson house, Mom said, reminded her of the train station in Chicago with people going in and out of every door at all hours, talking about food and showing off celebration attire and double-checking their plans for going to the party together.

But there was so much hugging—so much whispering things into Mom's ear that brought tears to her eyes, so much promising to pray for her and for Will and for Rudy—that Will was sure the food and costumes were just excuses so people could make sure Ingrid was all right.

By the time they all gathered in the Plaza, Will wasn't in the mood to celebrate. Despite the red, white, and blue bunting hanging from every adobe building, and the mariachi bands competing with one another from rooftops, and the presence of every person in Santa Fe and beyond waving little American flags and dancing in the streets—Will couldn't get out even one victory yell.

It's not over until I see Dad, he thought. *I can't celebrate 'til he's home.*

But everyone else in his group was so caught up in the festivities—even Mom, who was at that moment learning the cha-cha from Miguel—Will didn't want to be the one to, as Mom herself would have said, be a wet blanket. As soon as everyone was watching Mom and Miguel dance in the middle of the LaFonda patio, Will slipped away to the edge of the crowd.

He hadn't been gone 30 seconds when Fawn was suddenly there, twirling in front of him.

"So, you haven't said how you like it," she said, swirling leather fringe in every direction.

"Like what?" Will said.

"My outfit, brain child," she said, sounding to Will an awful lot like Olive. "This is a traditional Tanoan costume—it was my mother's, but the beads are my father's."

"It's nice," Will said.

"Nice? It's amazing! It means Quebi has blessed my parents' marriage. I can be Tanoan *and* Navajo and be proud of it."

"I'm happy for you, Fawn; I really am," Will said.

He plastered on the best smile he could come up with. She rolled her eyes at him.

"Who do you think you're foolin', Will Hutchinson?" she said. "This is me you're talking to—your sister."

"That's not exactly true," Will said. "My mom's not your mom anymore since you have your own family, so—"

His words were suddenly knocked out of him along with his breath as Fawn lunged at him, traditional costume and all. The pounding of her fists commenced and continued until Will hollered, "All right! All right—she's still your mom, for crying out loud!"

"And do you promise you will always be my brother and that you have never *stopped* being my brother?" she said, hot breath close to his ear.

"Only if you promise never to jump me again."

"That's askin' too much."

"Then just get off me now and I promise."

"Cross your heart and hope to spit?"

"Yes, for Pete's sake."

Fawn let go and bounced lightly to the ground, where she stood grinning, her beads only slightly askew.

"That's more like it," she said. "I'm going back to the party and let you keep praying."

"What makes you think I was praying?" Will said.

"Oh, come on, Will. You're always praying." She stopped and cocked her head at him. "You know what? I bet you're gonna be a pastor someday, which is fine with me, as long as you'll always admit I'm stronger and faster and trickier than you."

Then with a grin, she left him. But he didn't feel nearly as alone.

He was, in fact, working his way through the crowd to rejoin the group on the patio a while later when Miguel rushed up to him, out of breath and struggling for his English.

"Weel!" he said. "Come—a message has arrived for your mama. Come!"

"Message?" Will said. Even though Miguel was tugging insistently at his arm, Will slowed down, and he could feel his eyes narrowing. "What kind of message?"

"Yellow—you know—the tele—"

"Telegram?" Will said.

"Señora Hutchinson—your mama—she says you must come!"

Only because Miguel dragged him did Will get anywhere close to the patio. Even when he saw his mother at the table, holding the yellow paper, he wanted to turn tail and run. The crowd seemed to move slowly, as if it were all under water, and Will moved with it, until finally he was there, beside his mother.

"Sit down, Son," she said.

Will planted his feet. "No, Mom. Just tell me—just tell me what's happened to Dad!"

Mom grabbed at his hand, squeezing it with both of hers.

"He's alive, Will—he's alive and he's on his way to Hawaii." Her voice caught on her own laughter. "Your dad is coming home!"

Will could never quite remember, later, what happened then. It was a blur of hugs and shouting and crying that didn't untangle itself until the next morning, when Uncle Al called with more information.

"They found him and the other prisoners in the Santo Tomas prison in the Philippines," Uncle Al shouted over the static as Mom held out the receiver so Aunt Hildy and Will could both hear. "He's in Hawaii now being treated at the hospital here."

"Treated for what?" Will said. "What's wrong with him?"

Mom waved her hand for him to hush.

"I'm trying to make arrangements for him to be treated at Bruns," Uncle Al shouted, "right there in Santa Fe, instead of here in Honolulu. If I can do that, I'll have him home in a week. How would that be?"

Mom and Aunt Hildy Helen both shrieked. Will had to admit, later, that he did a little shrieking himself. When they all recovered enough to get back to the phone, Uncle Al was chuckling.

"I thought you'd like that," he said. "Now get ready. I'll call you back as soon as I have everything confirmed."

When he hung up, Mom could only stand there, the phone in her hand.

"Ingrid, you okay?" Aunt Hildy said.

Mom nodded. "I just think we need to pray," she said. "I've been begging God for almost four years. I think now we'd better thank Him."

They did.

The next week flew by as Will and Mom and Hildy Helen—and everyone else they knew—turned the dining room into a hospital room, with art supplies near the bed, which was turned so that Rudy would have an artist's view out the window. Mom and Will went to the Plaza and bought tooth powder and a shaving brush and civilian clothes. When they returned with them, Aunt Hildy Helen shook her head.

"What's wrong?" Mom said. "He won't be wearing a uniform anymore."

"I know, but you've been a little too optimistic about the size," Aunt Hildy said.

"He's always worn this size," Mom said.

"There are a lot of things that he has always been and done that aren't going to be the same, at least for a while. I think we might need to take a little trip over to Bruns Hospital so you'll know what to expect."

The field trip included everyone who would be close to Rudy when he came home. Aunt Hildy took them through the wards where men who were slowly trickling in from prison camps were recovering. Although they all greeted the Hutchinsons' group with smiles, Will had trouble smiling back for the lump in his throat.

Not a man there weighed more than 100 pounds, even those so tall their feet stuck out of the ends of the beds. Eyes were sunken into heads. Skin clung to bones so that Will could nearly see the blood coursing through their veins. Motions were jerky and random as they tried to wave.

"Dad's gonna be like this?" Will whispered to Aunt Hildy.

"He could be," she said. "I just wanted you to be prepared. But don't worry. He'll get better faster than these men will, because he'll be with you and your mom."

"And you—and Uncle Al—and all this family," Will said, nodding at Olive and Miguel and Fawn and the adults.

Aunt Hildy Helen smiled the so-much-like-Dad smile. "I was

right," she said. "That family tree was just what the doctor ordered for you."

Almost exactly a week after his first call, Uncle Al called again. There wasn't as much static this time, because he and Dad were now in California.

"I couldn't get through to you from Hawaii," he told Mom as Will and Aunt Hildy squeezed in to listen. "I didn't think you'd mind, though, if I bring him home tomorrow."

There was no shrieking this time. Mom just closed her eyes and whispered, "No, I don't mind."

"Be at the train station in Lamy at 5:00. I'll arrange for an ambulance, but have Doll Face confirm it, okay?"

"Who's Doll Face?" Will said when they hung up.

Aunt Hildy grinned two dimples into place. "That's me," she said. "He's been calling me that since the first day he saw me." She looked at Mom, her eyes shining. "Oh, Ingrid," she said, "we all have so much to catch up on. We can dream again now, just like we used to."

Everything was ready that night when Will went upstairs to bed. Even his clothes were laid out, and as he checked them for the tenth time for holes and spots and lint in the pockets, something suddenly occurred to Will.

I wear a whole different size than I did when Dad left, he thought. *I comb my hair different.* He put his hand up to his throat. *I bet my voice is even lower.*

And then another thought struck him, harder than the first: *What if I've changed so much he doesn't even know me? What if he doesn't like me the way I am now?*

There was something familiar about the thought, as though he had considered it before. It wrapped itself around him like tentacles and wouldn't let go.

Will crossed to his bed where his scrapbook lay open, ready for him to show it to Dad. But what if his father thought it was silly for Will to have kept such close track of the war? What if he was angry because Will was shoving the war in his face when he'd had more than enough of it?

What if Will didn't know what to talk about? What if he and Dad had been apart for so long they wouldn't know how to be together the way they always had?

Will crawled over his scrapbook to the window and looked out on Canyon Road. He felt as if his own thoughts would smother him if he didn't get air. The street was empty, except for two figures walking along the dirt road, heads bent together as they talked. Will grinned as the smaller figure suddenly jumped on the taller one's back and both of them shrieked.

"Good night, Fawn," Will whispered. " 'Night, Dan."

That familiar thought didn't strike him this time. It just eased into his head and made him sigh against the windowsill—the thought, the memory of Fawn on the back stoop, terrified that the father she was going to meet at the train station the next day wasn't going to like her anymore.

As Will watched them walk up Canyon Road, Fawn let out a loud laugh and Dan broke into a run, bouncing her on his back until they disappeared around the curve. Will watched long after they were out of sight. Would that be Will Hutchinson and Rudy Hutchinson, walking together, getting to know each other again?

There was no way to know. He could only hang on.

✛ ⬥✛⬥ ✛

Chapter Nineteen

*W*ill sat on a wooden bench with a carved back, shuffling his feet back and forth on the tile floor until Mom put a hand on his knee. It was hard to simply sit there. They'd arrived at the train station in Lamy early, and he had already read the timetable on the wall 20 times, checking it every few minutes to make sure he had the time right. Dad's train was still due in at 5:00 P.M.

Outside, the piñoned hills rolled toward the sky, as usual. And just as they always did, the ravens circled looking for food and the wind blew little gusts of dust against the window now and then.

How can everything still look the same, Will thought, *when everything is different now? When this is anything* but *a usual day?*

He couldn't help it. He started to shuffle his feet again.

"Why don't you go outside and walk around a little," Mom said, "before you drive me nuts."

She smiled at him, but Will could see that the edges of her lips were quivering. She was as nervous as he was.

"I'll tell you when I see it coming," he said.

He wandered outside to the brick-floored breezeway with its stuccoed arch and sat under it on a smoothed-rock bench so low, his long legs sprawled halfway out into the breezeway.

My legs are longer than they were last time he saw me, he thought, and then he swatted the thought away and concentrated on the sky. The breeze was almost-fall brisk. The sun was bright, the sky a seamless blue against the hills. It was never-ending—like this wait—

Will stood up abruptly. He'd been waiting since January 1941. Why did these last few minutes seem as long as that whole four and a half years put together?

More anxious thoughts crowded in. *Is Dad really on the train? Why hasn't Uncle Al called from a station along the way? They had to stop somewhere. What if the train's wrecked someplace?*

Will put his hands up to his ears until the thoughts quieted down, like students when they know the teacher has had enough. He waited for the Holy Silence.

Dan had been right. It was easy to come by in New Mexico, where the mountains themselves demanded silence and got it. In the quiet came the settled-in feeling he knew would come if he just waited for it.

It was the feeling that said, *Choose to hang on. It's the best choice. It's the only choice.*

Will wiped the sweat off of his palms on the fronts of his pant legs and licked the dry from his lips. Yeah, the silence was good.

And then it was jarred with the faraway blast of a whistle—and Will's stomach lurched and his mouth went cotton-dry all over again. He slid across the bricks to get to the station door to tell Mom, but she ran into him in the doorway on her way out.

"Mom," he said, "I'm scared to death."

"Me, too," she said.

There was another long-drawn blast of the whistle, half-screech, half-wail, and Will ran to the track and peered under the half-arch of trees that bordered it on their side, straining to see around the cruel curve that wouldn't let him see the train until it was right on them. The wait was maddening, right until the end.

And then, there it was. Will got as close to the yellow line as he could get, his feet stomping the bricks. Mom was suddenly next to him and the locomotive was suddenly snorting in, spewing out its gassy smoke and creaking wearily.

"Will?" Mom said.

Will looked down at his mother. Her face was the color of steam. "Hold me up, Will," she said. "Or I'm going to fall down."

Will put a clumsy arm around her shoulders and she sagged against him and groped for his other hand. She found it with her fingers, and as they clung to each other, Will realized for the first time that he was taller than his mother.

That was the way they were standing when the train wheezed to a stop and a face looked at them through a window and a hand rose to wave at them. Will felt all the air go out of Mom until only a whisper was left.

"Rudy," she said.

The conductor swung off the car and behind him came Uncle Al, stocky and grinning as he pushed his big shoulders through the people to get to Mom and Will.

"Take us to him, Al," Mom said.

"Doll, you just stand right here. I'm going to get the ambulance attendants to bring the stretcher." He searched the parking spaces with his eyes. "Is it here yet?"

"Al," said a thin voice from the train car door. "I don't need a stretcher. I need my family."

"Oh, my dear God," Mom said. "Rudy."

She let go of Will and ran to the ghostly man who tottered on the steps. He reached out his arms to her, and bone-thin as they were, he wrapped them around Mom and bent his head of curly hair over her.

He still has curly hair, Will thought as he watched them. *He's still taller than Mom. He still rocks her back and forth when he hugs her.*

Those were all things he'd forgotten. Were there more? He'd worried about Dad knowing him, but would he know his dad now? Had he been so busy growing up that he'd forgotten important things—things that were going to leave Dad disappointed?

And then he heard it—the thing he hadn't forgotten—his father saying, "Where's Willie? Where's my son?"

Those almost-five years slid off of Will like a silk shirt, and he shouted the word he hadn't forgotten how to say.

"Daddy!" he cried. "Daddy!"

He ran to Rudy and flung his arms around him and sobbed into his chest. He could feel Dad's face in his hair and his arms locked against his back. It was just the same as it had ever been.

Later, as Will watched the ambulance attendants help Dad onto the stretcher, amid the cheers and applause of strangers on the platform who were caught up in the homecoming, he saw that his father's waist was as narrow as a wasp's and that his neck was so thin, his head seemed too big for it. He wondered how Dad could have felt so strong to him in that first hug. Maybe, he decided, it was Dad's soul he was hugging—the part of him that even the Japanese war camp hadn't been able to take from him.

There was another homecoming when they got to Bruns Hospital. Aunt Hildy Helen was there, and she nearly collapsed when she saw her twin brother. Will was afraid she was going to go back into "shell shock," but a close look at her, even with the tears in her eyes, reassured him that she was going to be okay.

It was only a week until the doctors said Rudy was well enough to go home, as long as Mom and Aunt Hildy Helen followed the strict orders they gave them.

"They'll follow them all right. Don't worry about that," Dad told them, with the gleam that had already returned to his brown eyes. "I'll be begging to get back in here to get a break!" And then he looked at Will and grinned, the impish smile Will had seen every night when he'd closed his eyes. "You're going to protect me from them, aren't you, Son?"

"Yeah, Dad," Will said. "Now that it's even. There were *way* too many women here for one poor guy."

"Oh, poor thing," Mom said, lips twitching. They had, Will noticed, been twitching almost nonstop since Dad had come home.

The day of Dad's real homecoming was set aside as a quiet one, since simply moving from the hospital to the house was going to tire him out. But as soon as Mom gave the okay the next day, Fawn was there, present in hand, to meet Will's dad.

"So," she said, plopping herself down on the chair beside his bed in the dining room, "since Ingrid is Mama Hutchie, you must be Papa Hutchie."

Dad grinned at her. His teeth still seemed to take up too much of his face, but the brush of color was coming back to his cheeks. "You're a piece of work, aren't you?"

Fawn looked at Will. "Is that good?" she said.

"No," Will said. But when Fawn looked a little wilted, he assured her that it really was good—and then she jumped on his back just to show Dad how she handled Will.

Miguel and Olive arrived next—with gifts. Miguel was shy at first, but when Dad promised that they would talk privately sometime soon about Miguel's father, who Dad knew before he died, Miguel lit up and could hardly be persuaded to leave Dad's side the rest of the afternoon. Will waited for a pang of jealousy, but it never came.

Olive, on the other hand, looked Dad right in the eye and thanked him for the service he had done for the country. It occurred to Will that she might be making up for what her father hadn't done. But she truly seemed to like Dad, and she told him she'd been reading up on Picasso so they could discuss his work when Dad was up to it.

"How did you know Picasso was his favorite painter?" Will asked her later.

"Aunt Hildy Helen told me," Olive said. "She's so neat, Will. She said I could come visit her in Chicago whenever I want after she goes back there. I'm trying to talk her into *not* going back there."

"Huh," Will said. "It's like you have all these parents now."

"We all do," she said.

Will was disappointed that Dad would have to wait until Abe was out of the hospital to meet him. Or at least, he thought he would. But one afternoon in Indian summer, when Will and Dad were sitting on the front porch playing checkers, Bud drove up in the Chevy, pulled a fold-up wheelchair out of the trunk, and then opened the door to the backseat.

"What's he got back there?" Dad said.

Will let out a yell. "It's Abe! He brought Abe over!"

It was no small feat getting Abe out of the backseat, leg cast and all. But he was grinning his earlobe-to-earlobe grin as Bud wheeled him up the driveway and up the walk to the front steps. Dad went down to greet him, his legs steady and his arms actually showing some muscle as he gripped the rail.

"So this is Abe," Dad said. "I've heard all about you, my friend. It's nice to meet you."

Abe bobbed his head and put out his hand to shake Dad's, just as Bud had probably rehearsed with him a dozen times. But he kept his eyes lowered, lifting them only to shift them uneasily toward Will.

Dad cocked an eyebrow at Will.

"It's okay, pal," Will said. "This is my dad, just like Bud's your dad."

Abe nodded, but he still couldn't seem to bring himself to look at Rudy. Bud exchanged a puzzled look with Dad, and even Will was confused for a minute. It was Abe himself who finally explained it.

"What's wrong, pal?" Will said to him. "Come on, give."

Abe bent his head and muttered, "Will—come see Abey?"

"Come see you?" Will whispered back. "Of course I'll come see you. What are you talking about?"

And then it dawned on him, and he could feel his face turning red. "I haven't been to see you since Dad got home," he said. "Man, I'm sorry, pal. I guess I kinda lost my head, you know?"

"No," Abe said. "Abey don't know."

"Know this," Dad said. "I'm going to kick Will out of here tomorrow and make him get back to his regular routine. He'll be there the minute visiting hours start."

Abe grinned gleefully and stuck his hand out for Dad to shake it again, this time studying Dad's face and babbling away in half German, half English. For the rest of the afternoon, he did that several times, as if shaking hands with Dad were the most fun he'd had in weeks. For Will, just watching them was among the best things that had happened to him in the past four and a half years.

Once Dad was able to get dressed and sit at the table for meals and stay awake most of the day, preparations began for a real homecoming party. If Mom had thought the Hutchinson house had felt like the Chicago train station before, it was Grand Central this time.

Will was sure more food came out of the kitchen than he and Mom had eaten since they'd moved in—except for the time that Abe was with them, of course.

Margretta Dietrich and Conchita brought in flowers and Indian pottery for decorations, and Dan and Mr. T. strung up lights in the backyard. When the Lins arrived from Albuquerque, they brought Japanese lanterns to add to the festive air.

Will and Fawn were so excited to see Emi and Kenichi, their part in the preparations stopped temporarily while they caught up. But Will had to excuse himself to join Aunt Hildy in the attic, where they put the finishing touches on their family tree.

"Dad's gonna love this," Will said as they stood admiring the completed product.

"Yeah, but do *you* love it, that's the real question," Aunt Hildy Helen said.

"Me?" Will said. "Why me?"

"Because we really made this for you, Will—to pass down to your kids and for them to pass down to theirs." She smiled her dimples into place. "And you'd better make those kids of yours fill it in when the family expands, or Great-Aunt Hildy Helen will come in and give them the business. I didn't grow up in my Aunt Gussie's house for nothing."

The party was a huge success. People gathered in small groups in the yard, in the house, on the front porch, and Rudy went from one to the other, jauntily swinging his cane between leans, thanking people for all they had done for Mom and Will while he was gone.

Teachers from Will's school and ones Mom worked with at hers.

Reverend Weston and the people from First Presbyterian.

Friends they had delighted in at the Pink Adobe and the Plaza Café.

Bud and Tina and Abe.

Mrs. Lin, Yoji, Ken and Emi.

Miguel and Uncle José, Mr. T. and Señora Otero-soon-to-be-Tarantino and Olive.

Fawn and Conchita and Dan and Margretta.

Uncle Al and Aunt Hildy Helen.

Dad was still making the rounds when Reverend Bud asked everyone to gather in the front yard with their lemonades in their hands. He pulled Mom to one side of him and Will to the other on the porch and addressed the crowd.

"Rudy Hutchinson has spoken to every person here this evening, thanking us all for what we've done for Ingrid and Will in his absence." He looked down at Mom and then at Will. "But I think he needs to know about the things they've done for us."

"Here, here!" someone shouted.

Glasses rose above heads and the crowd of friends answered, "Here, here!"

"Without them, Mr. Hutchinson," Mrs. Lin said, "my children and I would have spent months more than we had to in a relocation camp."

"And either Fawn would be in reform school," Margretta Dietrich said, "or I would be in the sanitarium!"

Amid the laughter, Tina raised her hand. "I have Ingrid and Will to thank for discovering Abe," she said. And she lifted her glass to Will. He lifted his back.

"And would I have my new wife-to-be without these two?" Mr. T. said.

Señora Otero nodded. "I would have stayed wrapped in my grief and never have started life again. God bless you."

"Mama Hutchie's always gonna be my Mama Hutchie," Fawn said. "And Will's always gonna be my brother and let me jump on his back."

Will almost wished she would do it now. He wasn't sure he could take much more before his cheeks burned completely off. He even put up his hand as a final thanks, but Olive ignored him and said, "I love my new family. I'm going to be a Tarantino. But Will brought me to them—and if I had a second choice, I would want to be a Hutchinson."

"Who knows, Olive?" Hildy Helen said. "That's how Rudy found Ingrid—somebody who wanted to be a Hutchinson."

The crowd roared. If Aunt Hildy Helen hadn't produced the big framed family tree just then, Will might have pulled a Fawn and jumped her.

"Will and I have a present," she said as she pulled the blanket off of their masterpiece. "We made it for Rudy, but in a sense, it belongs to all of you."

Everyone crowded in, and a silence fell for a few minutes, the kind of quiet that happens when people are praying. And then the exclamations began.

"You traced your family back that far? All the way to Salem, Massachusetts in the 1690s?"

"Those Hutchinsons sure got around. Williamsburg, Virginia—Charleston, South Carolina—Chicago, Illinois."

"Look at all those different professions. You even had an actor in the bunch."

"I understand the branches," someone said, "but I've never seen leaves on a family tree before. What are those names on the leaves?"

"That's us!" Fawn cried. "Look—there's my name—and Miguel's—"

"Every one of us is on there," Olive said. "It's like we're all Hutchinsons!"

"Wonder who Nicholas Quincy was," someone said. "Back in Williamsburg."

"Get a load of these names from the 1800s," said someone else. "Tot. Bogie."

"Bogie was a dog," Will said. "Aunt Hildy knows all this stuff. She'll tell you."

"This is amazing, you two," Rudy said. His voice was tender with oncoming tears. "I am so proud to be on that tree—with all of you—with everyone who has joined our family through the generations. Reverend Bud, I think we ought to pray."

"Then let us," Bud said.

Heads bowed, and Bud prayed, and Hutchinsons and friends joined in with sighs and nods and the squeezing of hands. Will prayed, too—while looking at every face.

Every single one of us has been touched by the same war, God, he thought.

And every one of us is here because of the things that have happened in our families in all those years.

As the group prayed on, Will sneaked a glance at the Hutchinson family tree. There was one profession that wasn't up there. Maybe Fawn was right. Maybe he would be the first Hutchinson to become a minister.

The thought filled him up and he felt himself breathing hard. Beside him, Dad took hold of his hand.

It was late when everyone left. Mom and Aunt Hildy abandoned the dishes and went upstairs to bed. But Will couldn't go up yet. There was still something he had to think about before he could sleep.

He was sitting on the front porch steps when Dad joined him. The family tree was still propped against the wall, and Dad gazed at it before he spoke.

"What were you thinking while we were all praying?" he said. "You don't have to tell me if you don't want to—I just wondered."

"I want to," Will said. "Only I'm not sure."

"Let me give it a try," Dad said.

"Okay."

Dad leaned against the porch railing, his still paper-thin hands dangling lazily from his knees as he sat and pondered the family tree.

"You were thinking you're proud to be a part of that group," he said finally.

"Yeah, that's some of it."

"And if you're like me, you want to be worthy of it—you want to do something to keep the name of the Hutchinsons as true and good as it's always been."

"Yeah!" Will said. "Only I don't know how to do that. I thought maybe I should become a minister."

Dad's eyes took on a shimmer as he looked at Will. "Maybe you should," he said. "But whatever you do, as long as you do what every person on this tree has done, you'll live the life our Lord wants you to live."

"What did they do?" Will said.

"Exactly what you and your mother did while I was gone. Exactly what I tried to do with every man I shared those four miserable years with." He studied his hands as he went on. "I've thought about telling you about the horrors we suffered, the things we went through, but I don't want to go back there, Will—not even in my mind. What I want to share with you is maybe what you yourself have been trying to wrap words around." He ran his finger down the family tree.

"Every person here made the choice to believe in God," he said. "Every one of them chose to follow the guidance of Jesus."

"Our God who walked with us on earth as Friend," Will said.

"One of your dads told you that?"

"Quebi," Will said.

"I want to meet him," Dad said. "I need to thank him. He's been a Godsend—they all have. They've all pointed you right where I prayed you would go while I was in that prison, hanging onto my life."

"Where did they point me?" Will said.

And then he held his breath, because he knew whatever his father said was going to decide his life. Whatever he said was going to be true.

"Whatever you do in your life, Son," Dad said, "you have to make sure every person you meet has the chance to make that same choice—with nothing standing in the way—not prejudice, not hatred, not injustice, not ignorance. You have to open the way to God for everybody."

Once again, Will could feel himself filling up with something, and he breathed big breaths to give it room.

"That's a lot, Dad," he said. "You think I can do that?"

"You're already doing it," Dad said. He smiled at Will, like one man to another. "And you always will," he said. "You're one of God's Hutchinsons."

Then they were quiet in the Holy Silence and looked into the future.

⁕–⁑–⁕

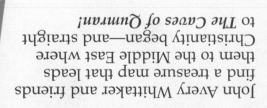

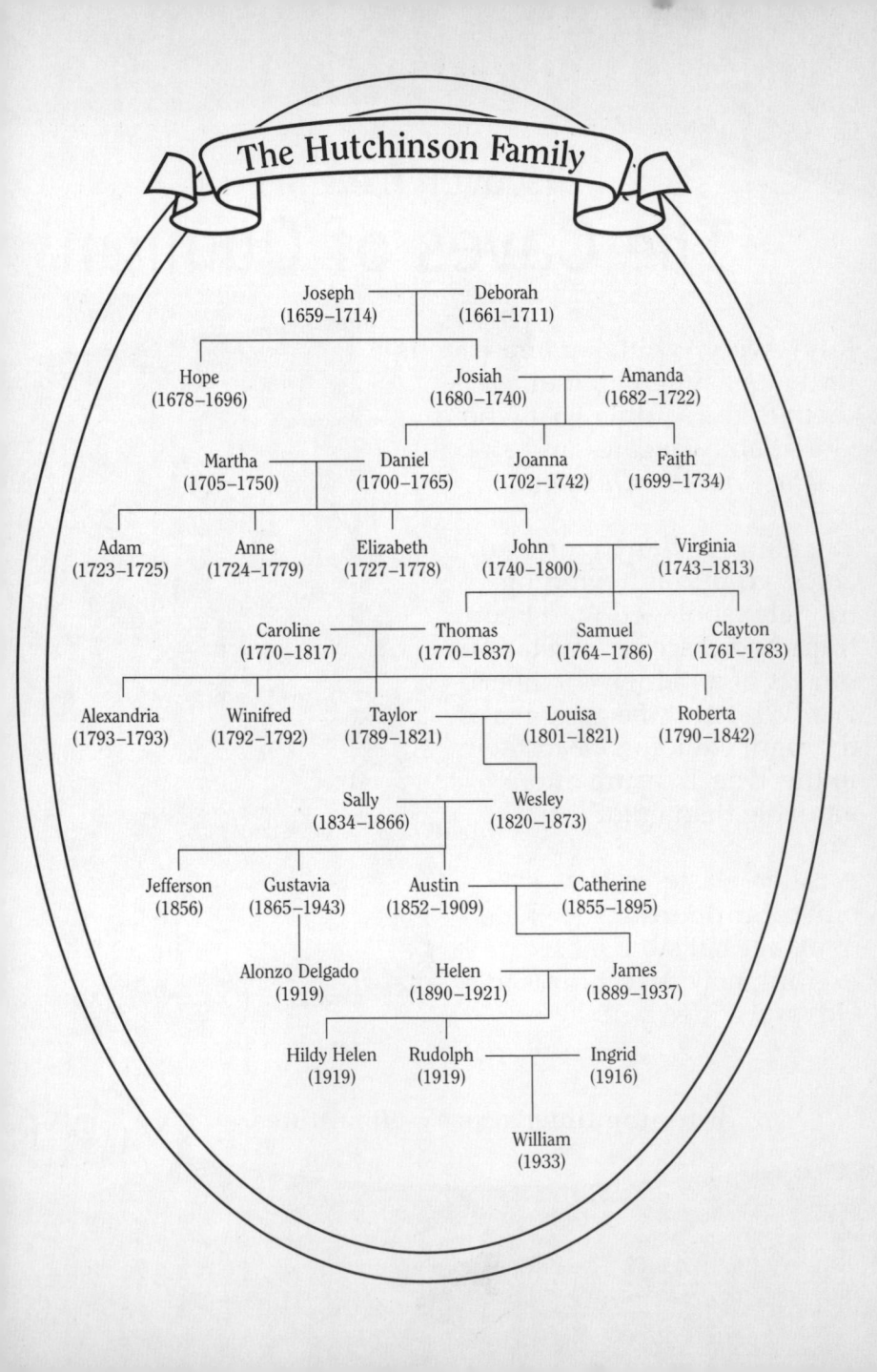

The Hutchinson Family

Joseph (1659–1714) — Deborah (1661–1711)

Hope (1678–1696)

Josiah (1680–1740) — Amanda (1682–1722)

Martha (1705–1750) — Daniel (1700–1765)

Joanna (1702–1742)

Faith (1699–1734)

Adam (1723–1725)

Anne (1724–1779)

Elizabeth (1727–1778)

John (1740–1800) — Virginia (1743–1813)

Caroline (1770–1817) — Thomas (1770–1837)

Samuel (1764–1786)

Clayton (1761–1783)

Alexandria (1793–1793)

Winifred (1792–1792)

Taylor (1789–1821) — Louisa (1801–1821)

Roberta (1790–1842)

Sally (1834–1866) — Wesley (1820–1873)

Jefferson (1856)

Gustavia (1865–1943)

Austin (1852–1909) — Catherine (1855–1895)

Alonzo Delgado (1919)

Helen (1890–1921) — James (1889–1937)

Hildy Helen (1919)

Rudolph (1919) — Ingrid (1916)

William (1933)